THE LOST TREASURE OF THE KNIGHTS TEMPLAR

THE LAST TEMPLARS - BOOK 1

PRESTON WILLIAM CHILD

INTRODUCTION

"True North" was the name Captain John Henry Holiday never knew he had. The men under his command only used it in his absence. It was their secret expression of their deep respect for him. Throughout their long, grueling training as America's most secret and elite combat force, they shouted what "True North" means to a "Shadow Warrior," whose existence was unknown to other Navy SEALs, to the nation, and to the rest of world.

"True North is the compass deep within that guides me! It defines who I am as a warrior

and as a human being! It's my fixed point in a spinning world! It anchors me!

It's my value and honor as a person, my strength and worth to my team!

No matter what decisions I must make, and actions I must take,

True North tells me the way I must go!"

Captain Holiday's team instinctively knew he wouldn't allow them to apply "True North" to anyone but themselves. They must always be inwardly focused by defining themselves as unique, irreplaceable members of SEAL Team Shadow. But Captain Holiday's team members also recognized he was their ultimate "True North." They'd feel adrift without him. To them, he seemed superhuman. As a surgeon and graduate of the U.S. Naval Academy, he was battle-tested and an inspiring leader, yet quiet and unpretentious. So as he wished, they just called him, "Doc."

The team's existence was classified, and they rarely set foot on U.S. soil. They lived and trained secretly in the bellies of Navy warships. Their presence was seldom known to more than the three highest ranking officers onboard. Team members had no family…no one to miss them. Secrecy drew them close to one another—and to their Captain. In battle, he was the rock that anchored them. Their conduct was moored to the example he set every moment, every day. His every thought was devoted to the team's success; he was fixated on each of its members and the specific missions. His every action set the standard by which they measured themselves. His every move determined their direction and pace. With him in their midst, they'd have no fear of defeat, and reveled in saying their inevitable victory was always "beyond a shadow of a doubt."

But August 2016 changed everything. Shortly before 10:00 a.m. on August 1, Eleanor Baird was dusting in the study of her home shared with her husband, Navy Captain Augustus Tucker Baird. She stumbled onto a secret panel in his big oak desk and uncovered a thin, leather-bound book. Thinking it might contain classified military information, her first instinct was to quickly return it to its hiding place, but a slight bulge in the binding piqued her curiosity. She opened the book and discovered it was her husband's journal. Specifically, the bulge was caused by her husband's slender, gold wedding band, which he'd never taken off during their 36-year marriage. The ring surprised her, but her husband's final journal entry shook her to her core.

"I'm not coming back," it read. "Tomorrow, I take command of the USS *Ronald Reagan*, the world's most powerful warship. We'll depart Yokosuka, Japan by mid-afternoon. Soon after, I'll deliver that instrument of death to the People's Republic of China. It's the will of God."

Eleanor dropped the book on the desk and frantically called her husband's brother, who quickly alerted the Yokosuka base commander, who in turn immediately called the Pentagon.

Those calls changed everything for SEAL Team Shadow. Doc was ultimately rocketed farther from True North than he'd ever been. And as the greatest adventure of his life unfolded, he held tight to his firm belief that nothing just happens...that everything happens for a reason.

1

INTO THE BREACH

I n the blackest hour, deep into the moonless early morning of August 2, 2017, three S-70 Black Hawk helicopters flew low and silently over the desert sand of eastern Oman, 40 miles northwest of Al Khaluf. Traveling at 110 knots, less than 30 feet off the ground, they soared side by side to ensure the sand they kicked up didn't obscure the air ahead. Two of the birds carried SEAL Team Warrior members. The third hovered alongside as a backup.

The crews and their passengers communicated with hand signals. The only sound heard as the birds approached their landing site was the low, muffled hum of their rotors and the "zzzzzips" of the Warriors sealing themselves into heavily padded, spherical, canvas drop bags.

Each Warrior wore a black jumpsuit and night vision goggles. Origin 12 shotguns, capable of firing 30 near-silent rounds in less than eight seconds, were strapped to their backs. Around one calf or the other, each Warrior wore a holstered .22 caliber Armatix smart pistol that could empty a nine-round clip in three seconds. Two Warriors, "Thunder One" and "Thunder Two," had a MAYHEM (Magneto Hydrodynamic Explosive Munition) slung over one shoulder that fired molten metal bombs able to blow 30-inch holes through armored vehicles and stone walls up to 18 inches thick. Team Warrior was ready for the firestorm that was merely minutes away.

Doc hadn't yet crouched inside his drop bag. He stood with his eyes locked on the chopper crewman who was preparing to open the bomb bay doors that would send the drop bags to the desert racing beneath them. When the crewman locked eyes with Doc and flashed ten fingers twice, the Captain gave a thumbs-up, squatted into his drop bag, and zipped it shut. The drop bags, tethered to the chopper's ceiling, gently bounced up and down on the chopper's floor to count down the final ten seconds before the drop.

Then the bomb bay doors fell open to the rushing wind and fiercely blowing sand below. As the team descended, thick nylon tethers slowed each bag's descent to reduce the risk of injury. The bags pounded into the desert floor and rolled approximately 50 yards before coming to a stop with their zipped hatches upright. Doc was the first to exit. He bolted upright in an offensive stance with his Origin 12 at the ready. His night vision told him the enemy (less than 300 yards away) still seemed unaware of their arrival. He slapped the watch's face on his left wrist, triggering the "Go!" signal his Warrior Team watched for inside their bags.

All eleven now stood tall, weapons at the ready. Only "Mountain" (a 6'6," 250-pound Samoan) struggled with the dizziness that always slowed him briefly during these drops. Doc waited just long enough for Mountain's head to clear, then waved the team forward. They silently sprinted through the sand until another wave from Doc sent them belly-crawling the last 100 yards. They stopped just 20 yards from their objective: a stone and steel compound roughly 75 yards square and surrounded by stone walls 18 feet high and 18 inches thick. Thunder One aimed his MAYHEM at the base of the wall directly in front of them. Thunder Two set his laser sight within six feet of Thunder One's, and the two of them waited for Doc's signal.

"Strike!" Doc shouted, and his team surged forward as the molten missiles rocketed into the wall. The Warriors breached the wall and fanned out, just as they'd rehearsed in a mockup of the compound for the past week. Thunder One and Two destroyed a pair of copters and a half-dozen vehicles parked inside the compound. Six other Warriors surrounded a squat, nondescript stone building at the center of the compound. Intel had told the team this was where the target code named "Twin Towers" would be sleeping. Doc was surprised when Mountain easily kicked in its heavy wooden door. Enemy fire peppered the sand all around the team. Inside the house, a solitary guard barely got to his feet before Mountain grabbed him by the throat. Then with his huge left hand, Mountain lifted him off the floor and slammed his head against the low ceiling. The move amazed Doc, and cleared the way to the target's bedroom. Assuming their prey was awake by now, Doc flipped on his back and kicked the bedroom door open with both feet, while the team stood clear in case they were fired upon from within. Doc leapt to his feet and led two warriors into the room, while Mountain and "Ammo" stood watch just outside the house's entrance. Doc and the others hand-cuffed and hustled the target into the courtyard, still half asleep.

Their captive's feet were unbound to allow him to run. His explosive necklace ensured he'd run in the same direction as his captors. Enemy fire slowed at the sight of their leader in front of the Warriors. Mountain and Ammo peppered the hostiles with Origin 12 shotgun shells to give the team cover. Eighty-three seconds had passed since the team had breached the compound's outer wall. Thunder One and Two blasted an exit into a wall opposite from where the team had entered initially. Flashing red beacons approximately 100 yards away told the team the three Black Hawks were in place.

Fourteen minutes after their drop bags hit the sand, the team was back aboard the choppers, bound for the Littoral Combat Ship, USS *New York*, and 20 miles off the southern coast of Oman.

"Twin Towers is your code name back home," Doc said to the captive in a low voice. "But your real name is Khalid Yasin."

"Khalid Mohammed Yasin," the captive replied defiantly with his chin raised.

"President William J. Preston sends his greetings and is eagerly awaiting your arrival in the United States," Doc told the captive. "But don't expect a friendly welcome. And when you're fryin' in an electric chair, remember Osama bin Laden. He ranted in his journal about how you and your cousin, Abdul, built the truck bomb that blew up under the World Trade Center in 1993. Some of my pals found that journal beside his bed when they sent him where you're goin'. So be sure to thank him when you see him."

"By the way," Doc added sarcastically, "you wouldn't happen to know where your cousin Abdul is, would you? We'd be happy to stop and pick him up. President Preston is eager to meet both of you."

"My father was at the Trade Center that morning," Ammo stated, with contempt.

"He should be burning in hell!" Yasin growled back at him.

"Well, he's safe in heaven now," Ammo shouted as he rose to his feet and stepped toward the captive. "So don't look for him where you're going!"

"Birds!" the copilot shouted back to the team as the choppers took evasive maneuvers.

"Ready the thunder!" Doc shouted into his headset.

The side doors of the two Black Hawks carrying Warriors slid open, while the third chopper entered a rapid climb as trained. Mountain and Ammo held Thunder One steady as he stood and took aim at the approaching enemy copter.

"Fire when ready!" Doc directed, expecting the thunder to begin.

But it didn't. One enemy chopper rose between the two Black Hawks, with another close behind. Thunder One and Two both feared their explosives would cut right through the chopper between them and strike their own birds as well. Doc immediately understood, so he covered the microphone of his headset and yelled, "Drop!" to his pilot. In a heartbeat, the pilot dropped the Black Hawk by

100 feet, giving Thunder One an upward angle that eliminated the crossfire. As Thunder One fired upon the lead enemy chopper, the follow-up craft pulled alongside it in the open door. The hostile craft also had its side door open, and a sniper had Thunder One in his sights. But before the sniper could fire, burning debris from the lead enemy chopper rained down, taking out the rotors of both the enemy bird and the Black Hawk. Thunder Two leaned out the side door of his unharmed ride to see the wounded Black Hawk fall toward the desert with six of his fellow Warriors aboard. As he made the sign of the cross and kissed the crucifix hanging around his neck, the third Black Hawk swooped down toward its falling twin.

The pilot of the crippled Black Hawk managed to crash-land it, burying the cockpit in the side of a huge dune. The impact collapsed the cockpit like an accordion, killing the pilot and his copilot instantly. Doc tossed his Armatix to the lone surviving crewman, while two warriors strained to open the side door, which had jammed shut upon impact. Doc knew enemy forces were likely converging on the site as Mountain swept his two teammates aside and yanked the jammed door open with sheer force of will.

As Doc had feared, armor-piercing shells began ripping through the fuselage just as Mountain opened the side door. Thunder One fired his last MAYHEM round into the darkness that concealed the enemy. Doc led the others in the direction of the third Black Hawk, now hovering three feet off the sand 100 feet away. As Mountain ran behind Doc to shield him, a single shot pierced Mountain's body armor at the small of his back. The Samoan released a scream and fell headlong into the sand. Ammo, and the warrior they called Grump, wheeled around and killed the sniper with simultaneous shots to his head. Doc pulled

Mountain off the sand high enough to heft him like a tree trunk onto his shoulders. The others looked on in amazement as Doc sprinted in the sand with the hulk across his shoulders, while enemy fire whistled all around him. They returned fire to cover their commander as he dumped Mountain into the chopper's side door. Grabbing both of Doc's arms, they jerked him onboard as the Black Hawk vanished into the darkness in the direction of the waiting LCS.

"I can't believe what I just saw," Grump admitted.

"Adrenaline's a beautiful thing," Doc replied between deep breaths.

"You're telling me," Mountain grunted from the floor of the chopper.

"Hold still," Doc said as he cut Mountain's vest loose to get a better look at his wound.

"You made me carry you for this?" Doc asked, pretending he saw nothing serious.

"I figured it was just something you'd always wanted to do," Mountain grunted back.

Knowing they were just minutes from the LCS, Doc quickly field-dressed the wound and checked the rest of the team's status around him.

"How's the other bird?" Doc hollered up to the pilot.

"She's aboard the LCS," the pilot assured him. "Our ETA is eight minutes."

"That's as fast as this bucket can go?" Doc shouted back.

"Write your congressman," the pilot snidely answered.

"Can you write, Doc?" Mountain grunted with a pained laugh from the floor.

"Delirium's setting in," Doc told the rest of the team, shaking his head.

Ammo had his eyes fixed on the captive the whole time.

"How's that necklace feel?" he asked. "I can tighten it if you'd like."

"Someday, Allah will have his foot on your neck!" Yasin growled back.

"Greater is He, who's in me," Thunder One said to Yasin.

Doc looked at his watch and saw the message icon. He rested a finger on the icon and a bold exclamation mark appeared.

"Calm down, men," Doc ordered, "we've got an urgent mission on tap."

"No rest for the wicked," Ammo said, and took a bite of the jerky he always carried.

"The wicked deserve no rest," Yasin spat at him. "They deserve…"

"Have some jerky!" Ammo interrupted him. "You're annoying me."

"Don't waste good jerky on this guy," Thunder One told Ammo.

"A bullet would do a better job of shuttin' him up!" Ammo spat back.

"At ease, men!" Doc commanded. "We've got bigger fish to fry."

"Bigger, but not as smelly," Ammo sneered.

"Enough, Ammo!" Doc demanded firmly. "Start prepping for our next mission."

"Brace for landing!" the pilot announced.

"You heard 'em!" Doc barked at Ammo and the others.

The moment the Black Hawk touched down on the USS New York, the team broke into a sprint and headed below deck. Doc ran alongside the medics who had Mountain on a stretcher and hustled him to sick bay. Doc stood by silently while a surgeon extracted a Russian steel-cased 39mm bullet from Mountain's pelvis, which it had shattered, causing severe internal bleeding. The surgeon lifted his eyes to Doc's and shook his head, as if to say Mountain's wound was a mess, but then nodded to assure him Mountain would make it.

Below deck, minutes later in a hollow in the bow, Doc found a Navy blue wetsuit and a can marked "Worms" lying on his bunk. He opened the can with his SOG Bowie knife and read the note inside.

"The President thanks you. Next: In the water at 0500 08/03. Destination: Sea of Japan. Bring no weapons."

Doc set fire to the note with his lighter and dropped it back into the can. He and his team had successfully completed nearly two dozen missions, but this next one was unique. The note gave no details, and there was no time for practice. There was also no room for questions, no time for confusion. Doc knew details would arrive along the way. So would the weapons. End of story. The other team members had wetsuits waiting for them too, and they knew what it meant. So the only briefing Doc had for them was that they'd have just four hours to sleep before they'd all be in the sea, headed for this next mission. The Warriors knew the absence of details meant this mission had the highest level of secrecy.

"Say your prayers and sleep well," was all Doc could tell them before he headed back to check on Mountain and let him know the team would be gone in a few hours.

"Can't it wait?" Mountain asked. "I'll be good as new in a day or two."

"Sorry, brother. Duty calls," Doc answered. "You're on temporary hold."

"Your odds of success would be better with me along," Mountain grunted.

"I know that," Doc confirmed sincerely. "But I also know everything happens for a reason."

"You're sayin' there's a reason I got shot?" Mountain asked contentiously.

"The most obvious reason is you're too big to miss," Doc laughed.

"So it was my fault?" Mountain snapped back at him.

"Everything's your fault," Doc laughed some more.

"Go get some sleep," Mountain huffed. "You need it…and you're pissin' me off."

"Calm down," Doc answered. "We'll be back before you know it."

"I'm counting on it," Mountain mumbled as Doc headed out the door.

2

OUT OF THE SHADOWS

The next morning at 0455, the half-dozen armed Marines standing guard below deck looked straight ahead as the Warriors hustled past. The guard at the stern ramp hit the switch to open it at precisely 0500. Dressed in their wetsuits, Doc and his team stepped off the ramp, into the sea. The Marines never saw them leave. As ordered, they and the rest of the crew didn't look in the direction of the approaching MH-60R Seahawk. So they didn't see it hoist the team out of the water and disappear into the darkness. Onboard the chopper, the team changed into sweats and the navigator gave Doc a quart-size can marked "Worms." Doc sat on a wooden chest and quietly read the pages inside for the next 15 or 20 minutes.

"Well, what's our mission, Doc?" Grump asked when he just could not wait any longer.

Doc looked up from the documents and fist-bumped a large button that dropped a soundproof door between the team and the chopper's crew. He held up a photo.

"This is Captain August Tucker Baird," he began. "Captain Baird is the brand spankin' new CO of the nuclear aircraft carrier USS *Ronald Reagan*. We're headed to the East China Sea to intercept and secretly board the *Reagan*. Take the good captain into custody and transport him to the US Naval Hospital in Yokosuka, Japan.

"Captain Baird assumed command of the *Reagan* just yesterday, at 0900. He set sail four hours later with orders to ready the ship and her crew for a routine, three-day Flight Deck Certification, which is set to commence at 0730, day after tomorrow. This morning, the Navy learned that Captain Baird believes God wants him to deliver the *Reagan* to the People's Republic of China. We'll stop him before he gets anywhere near China, sparing him—and the Navy—any embarrassment."

"If Captain Baird doesn't suspect the Navy knows what he plans to do, why don't they just order him to turn around?" Grump asked.

"The Chief of Naval Operations believes Captain Baird's lost his marbles, and that the Chinese government knows nothing about his plan," Doc said. "Our job is to keep it that way. Any questions?"

"Yeah, when does the fun begin?" Grump inquired.

"And exactly how will we secretly board one of the world's largest and heavily guarded nuclear aircraft carriers?" Grump also asked.

"ETA is just before the morning FOD walk, day after tomorrow," Doc maintained. "What's a FOD walk, men?"

"Foreign object debris, sir!" the Warriors all yelled.

"Why are they done?" Doc barked back at them.

"To eliminate material that might damage aircraft and personnel, sir!" they shouted back.

"Who participates in FOD walks?" Doc barked.

"All available hands, sir!" they confirmed.

"How many is that?" Doc shouted.

"A couple hundred or more, sir!" they barked back.

"Are they armed?" Doc roared.

"No sir!" they echoed.

"Roger that," Doc answered. "All available hands walk the entire deck of the carrier shoulder-to-shoulder, unarmed, picking up any and all foreign objects and debris. Everyone's attention will be focused on the deck surface immediately in front of them; a few may gab with those to the left or right of them."

"But that doesn't explain how we'll board the carrier," Thunder One pressed.

"Captain Baird expects an audit officer to arrive via chopper shortly before the morning FOD walk, to kick off certification activities," Doc explained. "But we'll be aboard instead."

"So how will we hold the crew at bay once they know we're aboard?" Ammo added.

"With the help of an old friend," Doc suggested as he opened a second, much larger chest.

"Thunder One…I'm sure you remember 'Lightning,'" Doc said as he lifted a hulking weapon—the Personnel Halting and Stimulation Response Rifle—into view.

"I remember it alright. It's totally unreliable," Thunder One huffed. "Half the time it didn't fire when we pulled the trigger. And it'd fire when we didn't pull the trigger."

"And it was supposed to stun your target," Grump huffed. "But it just made you see polka dots for a few minutes."

"That was a year ago," Doc countered. "I've seen it demonstrated throughout the upgrades. Our feedback helped perfect it. This isn't the same PHASR we used to laugh at," Doc said. "It's a whole 'nother animal."

"I'll believe it when I see it," Thunder One insisted.

"Do you really want to see it?" Doc asked as he pointed the PHASR at Thunder One.

"Wait…wait just a minute," Thunder One interrupted. "We knew a year ago that the UN banned this technology back in the '90s. Has that changed?"

"The ban only applies to use on enemy forces," Doc clarified. "Our mission is considered a test, using our own forces."

Thunder One took a good look at the rifle. It looked every bit as bizarre as it did when Warrior Team trained with it the year before—like something out of a science fiction movie.

"No thanks," Grump gasped. "I'll stick with my Origin 12."

"And I'll stick with MAYHEM," Thunder One said. "Our weapons are onboard, right?"

"It's PHASRs only, gentleman," Doc announced. "Remember, the ship's crew are all friendlies. So we will carry no other weapons and inflict no casualties."

"That's nuts!" Ammo spat out in disbelief. "There are more than 6,000 souls on board!"

"And every one of them is a friendly," Doc again reminded him.

"Are we at least allowed to inflict bruises?" Grump chided Doc.

"They're not expecting us," Doc said. "We'll be gone before they know what hit 'em."

"Wait! Wait just a minute!" Thunder Two chimed. "If we carry two PHASRs each, it won't be enough to accomplish what you're talking about."

"We have eight PHASRs," Doc exclaimed. "According to the plan, that'll be enough."

"C'mon, Doc," Ammo said skeptically. "You know we've always got each other's back. But this plan sucks. I don't care how powerful this new PHASR is, there's no way in hell eight of them will provide enough firepower against a crew of 6,000."

"It's the plan we've been given…and we'll make it work," Doc proclaimed.

"The guys at the Alamo at least returned fire," Ammo said, rubbing his shaved head.

"There'll be absolutely be no gunfire," Doc reiterated with stoic confidence.

"What are you thinkin'?" Thunder One asked in disbelief. "They'll hit us with everything they've got."

"They'll be unable to fire their weapons," Doc answered confidently.

"Why?" Thunder One shot back.

Doc stood the PHASR on his knee and unlocked the safety.

"Do you still want to see for yourself?" he questioned Thunder One.

"I guess s—" Thunder One didn't get his answer out before Doc fired the PHASR.

Thunder One instantly fell to the floor, temporarily blind and paralyzed.

"He's completely okay," Doc assured the others as he lifted and dropped Thunder One's right arm. "He'll be up and around in about 20 minutes."

"But how do we do that to 6,000 crewmen?" Grump questioned.

"This bird has the Mother of all PHASRs strapped to its belly," Doc advised. "Every crewmember who can see us—and some who can't—will be neutralized before we touch down."

"Okay," Ammo conceded. "But how will we find Captain Cuckoo in just 20 minutes?"

"Correction," Doc specified. "We'll have just 10 minutes. We'll need the other 10 to escape."

"I'm afraid to ask this," Grump said. "But how do we vanish in just 10 minutes?"

"Let's focus on finding our target first," Doc urged.

He held the can of "Worms" over the munitions chest, twisted the bottom of the can slightly, and it projected a deck-by-deck layout of the *Ronald Reagan*.

"Holy shit!" Grump exclaimed.

"The wonders of technology, gentlemen," Doc stated with a smile. "Captain Baird is a creature of habit. He's always on the bridge by 0630. There will be up to 16 crewmembers there with him, plus a Marine guard stationed at the entryway. And remember, they're all friendlies. And every single one of them will be blind, disoriented, and paralyzed."

"What about us?" Grump asked.

Doc reached back into the chest and hoisted a fighter pilot helmet with a full visor.

"You know, I'm not the sharpest pencil in the box," Thunder One admitted. "So let me make sure I understand the mission. We're supposed to engage and capture a disabled and blind crazy man on the bridge of one of the biggest, most powerful warships in the world, and then secure him aboard a CH-47 waiting for us on the flight deck seven stories below in under 10 minutes?"

"Piece of cake," Ammo murmured, still rubbing his shiny head. "But what I want to know is how we vanish in just 10 minutes. The *Reagan's* got state of the art radar, satellite communications, not to mention a couple dozen F-18 jet fighters."

"Don't worry, Ammo," Doc reassured. "We'll literally be hiding right under their noses."

"Now you've got my interest," Grady said.

"Well, it's about time," Doc encouraged with a grin. "Stay interested. I'll brief you and the rest of the team on that part of the plan later. For now, our mission is simply to board the *Reagan*, find and detain Captain

Baird, and return him safely to the U.S. Naval Hospital in Yokosuka.

"My next order is to get all the rest you can. The PHASRs weigh nearly 40 pounds and I haven't decided which of you will carry them yet. So sleep well and stay loose. We've got a long trip ahead of us and we're going to need all you've got when we reach the *Reagan*."

Thunder One finally awoke and rejoined them, rested and none the worse for wear.

"Hey, guys!" he declared casually. "What'd I miss?"

"Doc will fill you in, sleepyhead," Thunder Two chuckled. "How do you feel?"

"I feel great!" Thunder One replied. "I feel like I've slept for hours. We'll definitely not want to be around when the crew of the *Reagan* snap out of it."

"That's another purely temporary effect," Doc chimed in. "In another 20 minutes or so, you'll be as tired as the rest of us. So get comfortable and take advantage of the long flight ahead. Next stop: Viper Island, off the coast of Thailand."

Thunder One and the rest of the Warriors got as comfortable as possible and began preparing their minds for the mysterious mission awaiting them. It wasn't lost on anyone that Mountain wasn't with them. But they knew he was in good hands…and they were, too.

A day and a half later, while the Seahawk refueled and changed crewmembers at the White Beach Naval Base on Okinawa, Doc walked the members of his team through their respective assignments. The USS *Ronald Reagan* and its 6,027 crewmembers were sailing westward at 20 knots in calm, open water, approximately 40 miles south of the base.

"Ready your weapons," Doc ordered.

"Are you sure you won't change your mind about PHASRs only?" Grady asked, hopefully.

"Couldn't if I wanted to," Doc grunted.

"But would you, if you could?" Grump chimed in for a laugh.

"We'll never know," Thunder Two answered for Doc.

Refueled, the big chopper slowly lifted off the tarmac and headed east to intercept the massive, unsuspecting carrier. As the bird left the base behind, Doc spotted an incoming Seahawk. He suspected it carried the audit officer assigned to the *Reagan's* certification. That meant he'd likely be less than a half hour behind the Warriors when they hit the carrier's flight deck. So Doc knew the team must execute the mission flawlessly to avoid detection.

"We're on the *Reagan's* radar," the pilot called out to Doc 10 minutes later. "We'll have a visual in approximately five minutes."

Each member of the team knew his assignment. There'd been no time for practice or even a chance to get reacquainted with the PHASRs they'd soon have to rely upon to complete their mission. But that was all beside the point now.

As the chopper approached the hulking carrier, Doc shouted one last reminder.

"Remember, men! If you use a PHASR, it's because someone has seen us! So your target must leave with us!"

Neither Grump nor Grady had a PHASR. Their assignment was to be ready to quickly load any *Reagan* crewmembers brought back to the chopper.

The big bird now hovered 50 feet above the *Reagan's* flight deck. Approximately 300 *Reagan* crewmembers were gathered at the far end, watching and waving at the chopper. Another hundred or so were stationed at their posts throughout the carrier's island. As expected, Captain Baird was in the commander's chair on the bridge, along with the 16 crewmembers with various duties on the morning shift. A hulking marine stood vigil as sentry just outside. All eyes were on the chopper as it slowly descended to the deck below.

"Visors down, men!" Doc shouted to his team. "Give your best for God and country!"

"Lightning in three seconds!" the pilot roared. "One! ... Two! ... THREE!"

Even with their dark, almost opaque visors in place, the Warriors all reflexively blinked at the bright flash that filled the chopper's hull. Doc started the stopwatch on his wrist as the chopper's side door slid open, and he led his team out onto the flight deck at a full sprint.

As the Warriors ran toward the carrier's island, they resisted the urge to stare at the sight of hundreds of sailors strewn about the far end of the deck, as still as though they were dead. It was their first clue of the PHASR's upgraded power, and they were suddenly glad to have them. Running full out, the only sounds they heard were the chopper's rotors and their own footsteps. As they crowded into the island's elevator, Doc punched the "Bridge" icon.

"Remember," Doc insisted calmly. "Anyone you use the PHASR on leaves with us."

Doc silently prayed no such complication would occur.

Back at the chopper, Grump and Grady stood ready just outside its open door.

"If the team brings any crew with 'em, you take their feet and I'll grab 'em by their necks," Grump told Grady half joking.

"Guess this is where we get to bruise 'em," Grady laughed.

The elevator rose past the island's first six stories without a hitch, so Doc was certain the chopper's PHASR had done a thorough job as he and the team came to a stop just outside the bridge. The elevator doors opened, and the Warriors burst out, ready for the marine sentry. They were hoping he was unconscious. They found him lying deathly still against the entry to the bridge.

"Still tryin' to do his job," Doc grunted as he and Ammo moved the marine aside.

Not a single crewmember was visible through the bridge's large window, with the exception of Captain Baird, who was slumped over in the commanding officer's chair.

This is too easy, Ammo thought, and he sensed the rest of the team was letting their guard down and moving around too casually. He was sure of it when he heard Doc's voice…which never happened before under such conditions.

"Pick him up, and let's move!" Doc ordered.

For a moment, all was quiet. Ammo and Thunder One

lifted Captain Baird from his chair and Thunder Two hefted him into a fireman's carry.

"Where's Mountain when we need 'em?" he grunted and headed for the exit.

Ammo followed along to ensure Thunder Two navigated the narrow exit without banging the Captain's head on the way back to the chopper. Doc and Thunder Two's voices tipped off the *Reagan's* radar operator, who hadn't seen the PHASR flash because he was using the head. He'd become alarmed when the bridge suddenly went silent. Then, moments later, he heard unfamiliar voices, so he burst out of the head and crouched low to the ground with his semi-automatic .357 SIG pistol in position. Doc had his back to the sailor, who instantly fired two rounds into Doc's hip and upper left thigh.

"Damn it!" Doc screamed as he crumpled to the floor in agony.

Ammo dropped the sailor with his PHASR as Doc struggled to his feet.

"Bring him!" Doc grunted as Ammo and Thunder One applied a belt tourniquet to his leg and helped him leave the bridge with the rest of the team.

The Warriors froze in their tracks for a moment when they caught sight of the nuclear sub USS *Michigan* surfacing just 30 yards off the *Reagan's* port bow.

"Move it!" Doc shouted to them.

As they rode the elevator, Doc said, "Sorry fellas. I know now I should've told you earlier. If I'd been killed back there, you wouldn't know the *Michigan* is our ticket out of here."

"Where's it taking us, Doc?" Ammo asked.

"About 100 feet down," Doc grunted.

"But they'll find it," Thunder One said.

"They already know it's here," Doc grumbled back. "It's their escort sub. We'll lead the way back to Yokosuka. When the Executive Officer of the *Reagan* comes to, he'll be ordered to return the carrier to Yokosuka. They can search for us all they want. We'll literally be right under their noses."

The chopper made the short hop to the sub and quickly lowered the Warriors and Captain and their "guests" to the vessel. They then scrambled toward the horizon, with the crew of the *Reagan* none the wiser. The other chopper arrived just minutes later, with the expected Certification Officer aboard and unaware…until they touched down.

Ten minutes later, Captain Baird awoke and surveyed the team with groggy eyes.

"Attention!" Doc ordered his team and joined them in saluting the Captain.

"Who are you?" Baird asked. "And what are you doing aboard my ship?"

"SEAL Team Warrior, sir," Doc said. "We're here on behalf of the President, who's granted you some well-deserved R&R."

"That's ridiculous!" Baird shouted. "I've orders to ensure the *Reagan* is battle-ready."

"You're no longer aboard the *Reagan*, sir," Doc informed him.

"Where am I?" Baird barked.

"I'm afraid that's classified, sir," Doc answered. "Our orders are to ensure your comfort, while delivering you safely to the Naval Hospital in Yokosuka."

"To hell, you say!" Baird screamed. "I've a warship to command!"

"All you have to do for now is relax, sir," Doc replied calmly, pointing to a nearby compartment. "Grady, please show the Captain, and the sailor who so expertly nailed me, to their quarters and make sure they're both comfortable...and secure. Ammo, get the *Michigan's* medical officer down here to take a look at me. He'll need to check on Captain Baird, too."

"Aye aye, sir!" Ammo said and left in a flash.

Minutes later, the medical officer confirmed Doc's worst fear: The left side of his pelvis was badly damaged.

"I can remove the bullets and give you a transfusion," the officer told Doc. "I can do that onboard. But I fear you'll lose that leg if we don't get you to Yokosuka as quickly as possible."

"No dice, Lieutenant," Doc rejected flatly. "Our orders are that this tub will escort the *Reagan* back to the base as planned. Our team was never here. This emergency never happened."

Doc had the last word, of course. The *Michigan* and the *Ronald Reagan* arrived in Yokosuka together and neither crew ever understood what had happened. Captain Baird was admitted to the Naval Hospital for close examination and Doc's leg was saved, thanks to two complex surgeries over the next two weeks.

During Mountain's rehab, Doc learned Mountain had been medically discharged due to the damage sustained on their Oman mission. Doc tried in vain to reach his former team member by phone, but it seemed the huge Samoan had dropped off the face of the earth. More than anything else, this was the part Doc hated most about his team not having families. Doc feared he'd never find Mountain, if that was the way Mountain wanted it. But Doc vowed to keep trying.

Two months later, Doc, too, limped into civilian life and was forced to face the reality that he was of no further use to the SEALs—and the nation—he loved so dearly. He was referred to specialists at Walter Reed National Military Medical Center in Washington D.C. So he retreated into a small apartment 30 minutes south of the complex and two miles from the White House. Being in the nation's capital and around active military brought him the only comfort he felt. Unable to drive because of his injuries, Doc was a frequent passenger aboard buses, cabs, and the Metro. He walked often to strengthen his left hip and leg. As he regained his strength and flexibility, he began daily morning jogs. He soon became a familiar sight along the two-mile stretch between his apartment and Lafayette Square, just north of the White House. He jogged day after day, rain or shine, and clung to the thin thread of hope that he might someday be fit enough to resume a Naval career.

Doc imagined Mountain was undergoing much the same ordeal. Doc then devoted time each day trying to track the Samoan mountain down. But the truth was, Doc felt a little more defeated with each passing month.

3

CALLED AGAIN

Two months later, Doc awoke in Walter Reed Hospital following his third pelvic surgery. The time on the clock beside his bed surprised him. He remembered being wheeled to the OR at 0700. Now it was 11:15. Counting the half hour he'd likely spent in the recovery room, the surgery took far longer than he'd guessed. But it really didn't matter to Doc. As weary as he'd grown after so many days in the hospital and rehab, it made little difference how long this latest surgery had taken. Doc had no better place to be—not in the shape he was in currently.

Still drowsy from the anesthetic, he drifted in and out of consciousness for about an hour. He often squirmed in an effort to lessen the pain in his hip and lower back. Then he slipped back to sleep and dreamed of being in danger among shrouded characters who seemed familiar, yet eerily menacing. Everyone wanted him dead. Every attempt he made to escape resulted in greater danger. He struggled to fly a crippled helicopter over open water, through a howling storm, and desperately tried to find his way back to land. His engine was on fire and the fuel gauge was on "E." The whole time, some unseen enemy held the muzzle of a rifle to the back of his head. He slowly reached for his sidearm, but discovered his holster was empty.

Doc suddenly awoke with a jolt. The bad dream was like dozens of others he'd had since being wounded aboard the *Ronald Reagan*. But the dreams were becoming increasingly hopeless and threatening. The once-invincible Warrior secretly feared his mind and resolve may be weakening. Hoping to distract himself from such thoughts, he turned his head toward the sunlight flooding into his room, and finally noticed the tall, very fit stranger in leather, pressed denim and a Stetson standing at that window, looking outside at nothing in particular.

"Who are you?" Doc asked as he raised the head off his bed to a sitting position.

"Welcome back to the land of the living," the visitor replied, reaching into the inside breast pocket of his jacket for his wallet. "For a while, you had us a bit worried you might go to the big V.A. retirement home in the sky. You're a mighty restless sleeper, Captain."

The stranger opened his wallet, flashed a U.S. Marshal badge, and handed Doc his card.

"Quintin Marshall," Doc read aloud, and then snickered. "You're really Marshal Marshall?"

"Yeah," the visitor said with a shrug. "Life can be funny that way. Just call me 'Q'."

"So why would the Marshals Service worry about what happens to me, Q?" Doc asked.

"Let's just say, we represent a law enforcement official of the highest order who very much wants to meet you," Q replied.

"Really," Doc responded. "How high, exactly?"

"The top," Q answered. "He's invited you to meet with him at your earliest opportunity."

"He could've just stopped by himself," Doc replied, fishing for more information.

"That would require too much advance work," Q answered. "Background checks of hospital staff, Secret Service around the perimeter…you get the idea. Besides, I think he hopes the invitation serves to motivate you in your recovery. I suspect he's going to offer you a job."

"Well, I guess he's out of the loop," Doc said sarcastically. "I'm no longer in active service. I washed out months ago. Today's surgery was to clean up a few things from the other two. I'm really of little use to anyone."

"That's where you're wrong, Captain," Q replied, pulling a paper from the same inside pocket. "Men with your brains, skills, and courage are in high demand."

"That shows what you know," Doc mumbled as the pain in his hip and back worsened.

"We know enough," Q answered as he unfolded the paper and read it. "You graduated first in your class from Johns Hopkins School of Medicine at 20 years old. Four years later, you led the graduates of the United States Naval

Academy, just like your father, 35 years earlier. You could've coasted on the Navy fast track, but you spent the next three years as a SEAL, served with distinction around the globe, and earned two Purple Hearts, a Bronze Star, and a Navy Cross. I'm quite sure the United States Secret Service will make room for someone like you."

"The Secret Service?" Doc asked in surprise.

"I told you the invitation is from the highest order," Q replied as he prepared to leave. "Call me when you're ready for that meeting, and I'll make the arrangements," Q said. "In the meantime, rest and get your strength back."

Q paused halfway out the door and gave Doc a thumbs-up.

"I'll send someone to fit you for a suit in a few days so you'll look your best."

Alone again, Doc placed Q's calling card on the table beside his bed and looked out the window at the bright sunshine. He was still getting used to no longer being a SEAL. And suddenly, he faced the prospect of a very different sort of service to the nation. Just then, a very blonde, very attractive nurse swept into the room with a clipboard and a dazzling smile.

"Good morning, Captain," she introduced cheerfully. "My name's Connie. I'm your day nurse. How did you sleep last night?"

"Not well," he answered. "In fact, I was about to try to go back to sleep."

"You're more than welcome to," Connie replied. "But first we need to get your vitals."

A fresh-faced nurse-in-training, wearing brand new scrubs, came in right behind Connie, rolling a pedestal with a laptop attached. While Doc's arm got wrapped in a blood pressure cuff, Connie stuck a thermometer in his mouth.

"Sorry, but we still use the old-fashioned method," she told Doc with a glorious smile.

"How's your pain from one to ten?" she asked, looking into his pale blue eyes.

Doc lied, holding up three fingers.

"I'm good. I just need some sleep," he said, when Connie removed the thermometer.

"That's fine," she replied. "Lunch will be here in about an hour."

"Could you please tell them to send me a lobster tail along with the T-bone I ordered?" Doc jokingly asked, in the hope of seeing her smile again.

"I'll see what I can do." She grinned again and led the newbie out of the room.

Finally alone, Doc retrieved Q's card and replayed their brief conversation in his head. He was pondering the odds of anything resulting from the visit when the phone beside his bed rang.

"Hello," Doc announced, wondering who else knew he was in the hospital.

"Good morning. Is this Captain John H. Holiday?" a friendly woman's voice asked.

"Yes, it is," Doc replied.

"Please stand by for the President," she said and placed him on hold.

Doc sat up straight in the bed—shoulders back, chest out —and breathed in.

"Hello, Captain Holiday," John heard the President say energetically in his unmistakable voice. "How are you feeling this morning?"

"I'm fine, Mr. President," Doc said convincingly. "Never better. And you?"

"I'm doing fine too, son, doing fine," the President answered. "I understand you spoke with the marshal this morning. Did he tell you I'd like to meet you?"

"Yes, sir," Doc replied. "He sure did, sir. And I can assure you, I'm looking forward to meeting you, Mr. President."

"Well, I'm very glad to hear that, Captain," the President confirmed. "I'm eager to meet you, too. Tell me, have you given any thought to what you'll do once you've mended?"

"Not yet, Mr. President," Doc admitted. "It depends a lot on how well I mend."

"Well, you're in a terrific hospital and getting the best possible care," the President encouraged. "So I'm confident you'll make a full recovery. Once you do, I'd like to discuss a possible career move, if you're interested."

"If it's in service to the country, then I'm sure I'll be very interested, Mr. President," Doc said.

"That's good to hear, Captain," the President said. "I'll have the marshal arrange a meeting. You get some rest now. I want you healthy when we speak again."

Just then, Connie walked back into the room to retrieve the clipboard she'd forgotten.

"Yes sir, Mr. President. I certainly will," Doc proclaimed with a huge grin. "Thank you for calling, Mr. President. And thank you for the invitation."

"I'm looking forward to meeting you, Captain," the President said. "Goodbye for now."

"Goodbye, Mr. President…and thanks again!" Doc replied and listened to the call end.

"Was that the President?" Connie asked.

"Yes, it was," Doc told her, with his eyes fixed on the phone. "It really was."

"It's going to be hard keeping the other nurses away now," Connie mentioned with a chuckle.

"I'd appreciate your discretion on this," Doc expressed sincerely.

"I suppose so," Connie answered with another smile, "but it'll cost you a lunch when you get out. I expect to hear what that call was all about, too."

"I'm not sure I know exactly, just yet," Doc said honestly.

"Well, I'll still be here when you figure it out," she flirted and flashed him one more smile.

Doc leaned back against the upraised head of his bed and stared out the window again. He felt as though his life had suddenly gone from zero to sixty in one brief phone call. Now the pain medication was wearing off, reminding him that he was still stuck in the hospital for the next few days. But Doc's thoughts were now focused far beyond the pain.

He set his mind on mending and regaining his strength as quickly as possible. The call from the President changed everything. His heart and mind once again heard the call of duty!

Doc was now on a mission. He attacked rehab as though it were the enemy, and he was cleared for normal activity the same day his new suit, dress shirt, tie, and shoes were delivered to his apartment, just minutes from the White House. When Doc tried on the beautifully tailored suit, he found a note from Q in the breast pocket.

I figured since the suit is ready, you probably are, too, the note read. *Call me to discuss the details.*

Doc dialed the number in the note and Q picked up.

"Hey, Captain!" Q said optimistically. "How's the suit fit?"

"How'd you know it was me?" Doc asked, even though he assumed the answer.

"I know all I need to know," Q told him. "It's part of the job."

"Well, the suit fits great," Doc admitted. "Not too crazy about the tie, though."

"Trust the tailor," Q quipped. "It's a Preston tie."

"I know," Doc said. "I couldn't miss the label. But I'm a bowtie kinda guy."

"You got the right sense of humor, fella," Q laughed. "But you need to adjust your fashion sense."

"Maybe," Doc replied with a grin. "But I may not need a suit and tie."

"You'll need several," Q advised. "The President can be very persuasive."

"Most are, I hear," Doc answered. "So, what's next?"

"You're scheduled for lunch at the White House, at precisely noon tomorrow," Q reported. "I've arranged for a car to pick you up at 11:30. Please don't try to tip the driver. Enjoy your lunch. Hope you like Häagen-Dazs. Good luck, Captain!"

"Thanks, for everything, Q," Doc said. "I really appreciate this opportunity."

"Just doin' my job!" Q shot back. "It's great when your job is also your duty."

"Roger that," Doc exclaimed with a bold grin. "And Q... from now on, call me Doc."

"Doc Holiday," Q chuckled. "It has a distinctive ring to it, alright. I hope to see you again sometime, Doc."

"I look forward to it," Doc answered, ended the call, and saved Q's number to his phone.

At precisely 11:30 the next morning, a shiny, black Suburban pulled up in front of Doc's apartment building and double-parked. As the vehicle slowed to a stop, the well-dressed man in the passenger seat hopped out and stood beside the right rear door of the vehicle with one hand on the door handle. He looked relaxed, like he was supposed to, but his eyes rapidly scanned the surroundings back and forth, looking for anything unusual or out of place.

In the next moment, Doc stepped outside and the bright morning sunshine warmed him. He loved the way the suit moved with him as he descended the front stairs to the street. He felt odd having the rear door opened for him, but he also liked it.

"Good morning, Captain Holiday!" the man holding the door said to him.

"Good morning, fellas!" Doc replied as he quickly slid onto the rear seat.

As the Suburban rolled toward the White House, Doc scanned the front pages of the three papers stacked beside him on the seat. He wondered if any of the headlines would come up during lunch. He made a point of skimming over all three, but figured his demeanor was going to count for more than the morning news. Doc's watch said 11:40 when the Suburban pulled up to the north entrance of the White House, where two young, well-scrubbed marines in impeccable uniforms stood to attention and saluted even before the gleaming vehicle came to a stop in front of them. The front seat passenger quickly hopped out again and opened Doc's door as though he'd practiced the move endlessly.

"Good morning, Captain Holiday!" the marine on the right declared as Doc stepped out.

"Welcome to the White House, sir!" the marine on the left said warmly.

"Good morning, men! Looking good!" Doc commended sincerely as he returned their salutes.

The marines escorted Doc through the north reception room, past two silent secret service agents, and up the Truman staircase to the first family's private residence on the second floor. For the first time since the President's phone call to the hospital, Doc was nervous. Though Doc had spoken to more than a few high-ranking officers and undertaken missions of great importance to the nation, he'd never been this close to the ultimate power of the entire world.

"Get a grip, sailor," Doc silently told himself as the marines led him down the long hallway and through the double doors that led to the first family's private residence.

"The President will be with you momentarily," one of the marines mentioned, and they both left.

The furniture looked comfortable, but Doc wanted to be standing when the President entered. So he moved to the nearest wall and admired a stunning oil painting of the first lady until President Preston strode into the room with a warm grin and extended his hand.

"Finally, we meet, Captain Holiday!" the President expressed cheerfully. "Nice tie, by the way!"

"Thank you, Mr. President," Doc said. "It's my favorite."

"I'm starving!" the President announced. "How about you? Let's move into the other room and get comfortable."

Doc followed the President into a cozy drawing room, with a small table set for two. A waiter stood silently nearby.

"Have a seat, Captain," the President said. "What would you like to eat?"

"Well, what do you have, Mr. President?" Doc asked.

"You name it, we probably have it," the President boasted. "Personally, I'm up for a sirloin burger, fries, and a Diet Coke. How about you?"

"That sounds great!" Doc said, looking at the waiter, who was already moving slowly in the direction of the kitchen. "Medium-well on the burger, please."

Doc was grateful to find it so easy to relax in the President's presence. Doc was thrilled that his rehab therapy had greatly relieved the pain that once prevented him for sitting still for more than a few minutes.

"Thanks so much for coming," the President confirmed graciously. "I've looked forward to meeting you. I must say, I'm sure your parents would be quite proud of your excellent service to our country. You're a hero," the President said. "A genuine hero! But I suppose only a few people will ever be aware of it. I don't know if you know this, but I knew your father…both your father and your mother, actually."

"No, I didn't know that," Doc answered excitedly. "How did you come to know them? I'd love to hear that story."

"Your parents were good friends with my mother and father," the President alleged. "My father once told me that he met your father and mother in the mid-1960s, when they rented an apartment in a development my father built and managed near the Brooklyn Navy Shipyard. Your father wasn't a SEAL yet and your mother was writing her very first book. They often visited my parents before your father shipped out to Vietnam. I actually sat at the supper table with both of our parents a number of times. I remember your mother talking about her book and ideas she had for others. And your father had fascinating stories about the Navy—and his plans to become a SEAL. That was before I went off to the Wharton School at the University of Pennsylvania in '66. Now, here we're having lunch together half a century later."

"Wow!" Doc disclosed with a smile. "That's amazing! I recall my parents mentioning yours a time or two when I was young, but I never realized they were good friends. I'm sure I would've known had they lived longer."

"Yes, I'm sure you would have," President Preston said. "I'm truly sorry you didn't have more time with them. I only made the connection to you when your service file landed on my desk not long after you were released from active duty. How are you feeling by the way?"

"I'm great! Chomping at the bit!" Doc suggested, as he'd rehearsed most of the morning.

"That's tremendous!" the President said. "You look like you could run a marathon."

"Well, I'm not ready for that," Doc blushed. "But I could be, with time to train."

Just then, the waiter rolled a cart loaded with lunch to the table and served them.

"So," the President articulated, matter-of-factly, "I'd love to have you on my Secret Service detail. I know our fathers would feel the same way. The uniform's not as fancy as the Navy's. But the pay and benefits are pretty good and you can still see the world. To be totally honest, I'd be more comfortable having your medical knowledge within arm's reach. You never know what could happen. So it's a 'win' for both of us. Whadaya say?"

"Sounds like quite a career move," Doc acknowledged, "if I can make the cut."

"You'll do fine," the President confirmed, shaking Doc's hand. "Welcome aboard, Captain!"

"Since I suppose we're going to be seeing a lot of each other," Doc suggested warmly, "please call me Doc."

"Okay, Doc. Let's eat!" the President said with his arms open wide and his tie tossed over one shoulder to avoid stains.

4

THE REASON

To Doc's surprise and relief, he made it through Secret Service basic training easily and was immediately assigned to the President's detail. He served with the same commitment and dedication he'd demonstrated as a SEAL. Wherever the President went, Doc followed. At the White House, Doc typically stood just outside the doors of rooms the President occupied. When the President was on foot in public, Doc always walked just to the leader's right. In motorcades, Doc rode along in Cadillac One, the Presidential limousine, a.k.a. "The Beast." When off duty, he frequently checked in with the agents guarding the President.

Doc's SEAL training, and having been shot twice in the line of duty, made him ever-vigilant. No matter how routine and placid circumstances seemed, Doc was never bored into distraction or carelessness. The President appreciated the assurance that Doc was more than capable, and practically omnipresent. For his part, Doc appreciated the President's obvious allegiance and faith in his abilities.

So it was no surprise among Doc's colleagues that he was the first Secret Service agent to be shot in the line of duty in the 21st Century. Fortunately for the President, Doc had rescheduled a vacation in order to accompany him to a rally in downtown Detroit. Unfortunately for Doc, the single bullet fired by the would-be assassin as Doc wrestled the pistol away from him, struck his third lumbar vertebra, and lodged so deep within it the surgeons decided not to remove it.

The one bright spot in the ordeal was that Doc landed back in Walter Reed…and Connie was still there.

"Well, Captain," she remarked as she walked into his room the first afternoon. "Did you ever figure out what the President called you for the last time you were here?"

"I did," he answered and rubbed the back of his neck. "That's how I ended up back here."

"He shot you?!" Connie exclaimed in mock horror. "We'll block his calls from now on!"

"Please don't," Doc chuckled. "Knowing him, he'll show up here if you do."

"So you two are close?" Connie asked sincerely as she inserted a thermometer under Doc's tongue.

"You could sshhhhay that," Doc slurred back at her.

"I know it," Connie gushed with her trademark smile as she noted Doc's temperature on her clipboard. "I watch the news, and I saw you save his life. You're a genuine hero, Captain."

"That and two dollars will buy me a decent cup of coffee," Doc answered softly.

"Speaking of buying coffee, you owe me a lunch," Connie reminded him with her best smile.

"I guess you're right," Doc said. "How's the cafeteria here?"

"Oh, no you don't," Connie pointed a finger at him. "I was very clear that you'd have to buy me lunch when you got out of here the first time. But you slipped out when I was off. You probably thought you'd gotten away scot free. Well, here you are back again, and I'll keep a closer eye on you this time."

"Okay…but I don't plan to be here long," Doc lightheartedly advised her.

"You didn't plan on being back here at all," she reminded him, "and look how that went."

"You got a point there," Doc confessed, and they both laughed.

Doc liked everything he knew about Connie: her looks, her sense of humor, her caring manner…and most of all, her amazing smile. And he knew he wanted to get to know her better.

"Okay, I give up," he said with raised hands. "Lunch is on me, when I'm released."

"You bet it is," Connie shot back as she headed to the next patient.

After Connie made her exit, Doc's heart and mind wrestled with the reality that he was headed for his second medical retirement in less than a year. Dark thoughts had dogged him since he learned the bullet was in his spine permanently. His head spun when he thought about it. So he did his best not to dwell on it. Seeing Connie had briefly taken his mind off the mess the bullet had made of his plans, so that was reason enough to want her around. However, it wasn't his only motivation, but he knew he was in no position for a relationship. He struggled with periodic limited movement in his left leg and hand, which sometimes made simple tasks like opening jars and putting one foot in front of the other very difficult. So he didn't expect to have any job prospects for a while.

Doc was acutely aware that he'd be difficult to be around if he didn't have something to do very soon. Just as Doc felt himself begin a slow, downward spiral toward self-pity, his cell phone rang. It was the White House.

"Hello, Mr. President," Doc greeted warmly.

"Hello, Doc!" the President said. "How are you? I hope they're taking good care of you."

"They are, Mr. President," Doc replied. "But I'll be happy to get out of here soon."

"Don't rush it, Doc," the President answered. "I just got a full report and I'm very sorry to hear the news about your injury. But I understand you're going to be fine and that you'll be up and around soon."

"I pray you're right, sir," Doc answered. "I don't handle lying around very well, not when I don't have any idea when it'll end."

"Well, as far as I'm concerned, it'll end as soon as you're willing and able to get back to work."

"Well, the report you received must not be accurate, sir," Doc clarified. "The doctors have made it clear that my action-packed days are over."

"Oh, I don't doubt that," the President assured him. "But our nation still needs your knowledge and experience. I've asked around and I believe I've just the ticket to convince you to return to work at the White House. Are you interested?"

"Is this another lunch invitation?" Doc asked with a grin.

"Whenever you're ready!" the President replied.

"Will it be alright if I bring a guest?" Doc asked hopefully.

"Of course," the President quickly answered. "I've asked to be notified when you're released to return home. I'll expect a call from you once you settle in. How's that?"

"That's great, Mr. President," Doc proclaimed happily. "Thanks for calling, sir."

"It's my pleasure, really, Doc," the President reiterated. "Being the very grateful benefactor of your courage and fast action, it's an immense comfort for me to hear your voice sound so strong."

"Goodbye, sir. And thanks again," Doc stated and listened to the call end.

Not long afterward, just as Doc was dozing off to sleep, a familiar face stood in the doorway to his room and knocked lightly on the door jamb.

"Marshal Marshall!" Doc blinked and called out, no longer drowsy.

"How ya' doin', Doc Holiday?!" Q asked as he crossed the room.

"I'm fine," Doc lied. "And I'll be better if I can just get people to stop shooting me."

"Yeah, I heard," Q said. "Folks tell me you're quite the hero."

"There's got to be an easier way," Doc chuckled and groaned and rolled left, then right, trying to ease the pain in his back.

"If you find one, take it," Q replied. "So how are you really doing, Doc?"

"I'm okay, Q. Really," Doc sighed. "There's nothing wrong with me that having a bullet removed won't fix."

"I heard that part, too," Q confirmed as he pulled a chair to Doc's bedside. "Have you ever given any thought to finding a safer line of work?"

"Funny you should ask," Doc mentioned. "The President called just a little while ago to say he thinks he has another job for me."

"Guess I'm out of the loop this time," Q admitted. "What sort of job is it?"

"Don't really know yet," Doc answered. "But I'll know soon enough."

"Well, I'm sure you're the perfect person for the job," Q stated. "The President has a real knack for picking the right people to get things done."

"I hope you're right, Q," Doc alleged. "But I really don't know what's around the next bend for me."

"Come what may, Doc, I just hope you'll be happy and healthy," Q suggested. "You're quite a guy, and I wish we'd met under better circumstances. If I had known that helping to onboard you last time was going to land you here, I would've run the other way."

"S'okay Q. Really," Doc claimed. "Everything happens for a reason. I truly believe that. I can't always understand the reason…but I know there always is one."

"Maybe you're right," Q replied. "I've spent my whole life dealing with the things that happen. Still do. I've never really taken the time to look for the reasons."

"Give it a try sometime, Q," Doc advised. "If you're payin' attention, the reasons eventually become obvious."

"I'll remember that, Doc, I really will," Q acknowledged and headed for the door. "Gotta' go. But I'll stay in touch. Be well and get home soon, my friend."

"You be well also, Q," Doc replied. "Thanks for coming by!"

Q almost bumped into Connie on his way out of Doc's room.

"Pardon me, miss," he apologized, tipping his Stetson.

"Ahhh! No problem!" the flustered nurse told the handsome stranger.

Connie led another "newbie" into Doc's room with another laptop on a pedestal.

"Who's your friend?" she asked, trying to sound nonchalant.

"That was U.S. Marshal Marshall," he announced with a grin.

"Who?" Connie said with a squint.

"Just call him 'Q'," Doc offered, eager to monopolize her attention.

"Good news!" Connie suggested with one of her best smiles. "The surgeon says you should be able to go home in a couple of days if there are no complications, and you're able to walk and use the bathroom unassisted."

"That's GREAT news, nurse!" Doc remarked in his happiest voice of the day. "I'll work on the bathroom part privately. But I'll count on you to keep the complications away."

"Call me Connie...please," she replied. "I feel we're friends by now."

"Then call me Doc," he told her.

"Rrrreally?!" Connie asked with a clear tone of doubt.

"It's a long, boring story," he assured her.

"As I recall, you've a few stories to tell me," Connie replied. "So when's lunch?"

"Get me out of here and I'll take you anytime you'd like," Doc answered.

"It's a deal," she smiled back. "And just where do you plan to take me?"

"How's the White House sound?" he suggested with a beaming smile.

"Do...do you mean the White House?" Connie asked off balance.

"I just got the invitation from the President himself," Doc answered.

"I'll have to buy a new outfit," Connie thought out loud.

"I was hoping you didn't plan to wear your scrubs," Doc

joked. "Not that they don't look great on you. It's just that I don't want to look like more of an invalid than I already do."

"Very funny, Doc," she sighed with an eye roll. "Real cute."

"There's something you can explain for me…if you don't think I'm being too nosy," she coaxed.

"Shoot," Doc assured her.

"Your chart doesn't list any next of kin," she said.

"Don't have any," Doc confirmed simply, with a shrug.

"So how does an orphan achieve as much as you have?" she asked earnestly.

"Well, of course, it's not that simple," Doc explained. "My parents married relatively late, and had me after years of trying. Then they died in a plane crash when I was in grade school. Neither of them had any living relatives. My father was a doctor and a Navy SEAL. My mother was a popular gothic romance novelist. So they left me a small trust fund and a few connections who helped me along the way. But with no living relatives, I ended up in foster care with an older, childless couple who were wonderful to me growing up. But by the time I was in med school, they had both died.

"When I graduated, I served my residency in the Navy. Eventually, I signed up for SEAL training and made the cut. I can't tell you most of the rest, but it's pretty boring anyway."

"Oh, I'm sure it is," Connie mentioned, feigning agreement. "I mean, all of our patients have U.S. Marshal friends who visit them and get invitations from the President."

"Listen, Connie. If I didn't believe everything happens for a reason, I'd say my life was just a series of very lucky breaks...except for my parents dying, that is," Doc stated flatly.

"Do you really believe everything happens for a reason?" Connie pressed him.

"I do," he shot back.

"So why were you shot?" she pressed some more.

"This time? Or are you asking about all the other times, too?" he teased her.

"Let's start with this time," she answered seriously.

"I didn't say I know the reason," Doc finally conceded. He pointed to the Bible lying on the table beside his bed and told her, "I just know there is a reason. Proverbs 16:9 says, 'A man's mind plans his way, but the Lord directs his steps.'"

"And you honestly believe that?" Connie continued pressing.

"With all my heart," Doc shot back. But the next thing out of his mouth surprised even him. "So if I had to guess right this minute...I'd say I was shot so that I'd meet you."

Connie blushed deeply and looked at her shoes for a long moment before responding.

"That's the nicest thing anyone's ever said to me," she confessed softly. "Weird...but nice."

"Well, only time will tell if there are other reasons as well,"

Doc said. "But I'm sure that's one of 'em. But enough of the small talk," Doc said, changing the subject. "How soon can you get me out of here?"

"Hey! Were you just sweet-talking me?" she asked light-heartedly.

"No. Honest," Doc answered sincerely. "But the sooner I get out of here, the sooner you get to meet the President and enjoy lunch at the White House."

"Since you put it that way, I forgive you," Connie softened even more. "I'll see what I can do. But you have to do your part, too…starting with walking to the bathroom by yourself."

"So I ask you"—Doc spread his arms in a grand gesture —"is my life glamorous, or what?"

5

AN AMAZING OPPORTUNITY

D oc soon managed his first walk, but with considerable difficulty. Q called to check on him the next day and Connie shared a story of Doc almost falling. So on his next visit Q brought Doc a hand-carved, mahogany cane.

"What am I supposed to do with this?" he asked Q, with a trace of disdain.

"Well, I don't know," Q said, playing stupid. "What do folks usually do with canes?"

"I need a cane like I need a hole in the head," Doc huffed.

"Well, you do have that," Q said flatly. "I just thought you would know that canes are classy. All rich people have at least one cane."

"I can't think of one," Doc sarcastically challenged him.

"That's because you don't know the right people," Q chided him. "Bat Masterson carried a cane, for cryin' out loud. So did the real Doc Holliday. I figure you'll fit right in."

"Masterson was a dandy. Earp was disabled. I'm neither," Doc exclaimed in exasperation.

Connie walked into the room at that moment and teased, "If you ask me, you're both."

"Well, nobody asked you," Doc glibly replied. "It's a nice cane, though."

"Let's see if it helps steady you," Connie encouraged Doc.

He slowly slipped off the bed and touched the cane to the floor. He walked to the door of his room, paused just long enough to smile at Connie and Q over his shoulder, then turned right and walked in the direction of the elevator.

"Whoa, big fella. Where do you think you're going?" Connie asked, running after him.

"This ain't half bad," Doc suggested, wagging the cane. "Think I'll go down to the cafeteria."

"Q, will you please go with him?" Connie asked the marshal.

"Yeah, but not with his gown untied in the back the way it is," Q told her.

"You gotta help me with that, partner," Doc chuckled and faced away from Q.

"The things I do for you..." Q grumbled and tied the gown as the elevator opened.

From then on, Doc kept the cane handy. The next day, Q brought the maker of the cane with him to inlay Doc's golden trident into the handle. He worked silently, with a single carving tool. When he finished, the dark, shiny, hardwood cane with its golden inlay was a work of art.

"It's beautiful," Doc praised as he hefted it into the sunlight coming through his window. "I was a little insulted when you first brought it to me. Now I don't know what to say. Except thank you very much."

"The look in your eyes says it all, Doc," Q said. "You're very welcome, my friend. Do you ever watch that TV?" Q asked, pointing to the flat screen high on the wall opposite Doc's bed.

"Sometimes," Doc confessed. "If there's something worth watching."

"Well, it's nearly 3:30," Q said, glancing at his watch. "Do you mind if I watch SpaceX launch its first Falcon Heavy rocket?"

"SpaceX? Isn't that the outfit owned by Elon Musk?" Doc asked.

"It is," Q replied as he turned the TV on and found coverage of the launch.

"That's a monster rocket!" Doc said.

"The biggest and most powerful since the Saturn V," Q said. "And he's got one of his Tesla Roadsters in the cargo bay."

"You're kidding," Doc responded.

"Not at all," Q remarked. "Musk is attempting to put one of his cars into orbit around the sun."

"Boy, that'll break the 'miles traveled' record," Doc laughed.

"Yeah, without adding a single mile on the odometer," Q snickered too.

Doc and Q were riveted to the TV throughout launch operations that afternoon. Doc was overwhelmed when the huge Falcon Heavy's twin boosters returned to the launch site simultaneously and landed upright, ready to reuse.

"That's the most incredible thing I've ever seen!" he admitted.

"Me too," Q agreed. "They're launching rockets every few weeks now."

"Sounds very expensive. What's he up to?" Doc inquired.

"He's in a race with several other private companies for huge NASA contracts," Q told him. "They're all predicting there'll eventually be billions and billions of dollars to be made lifting U.S. and foreign satellites and crews into Earth's orbit and beyond. NASA has essentially privatized the nation's launch capabilities, saving the government billions of dollars in costs and getting out of the way of rich guys who have stardust and dollar signs in their eyes. President Preston's a big fan of space exploration and wants the nation back in the business of space exploration. So he's waving huge government subsidies at private rocket builders, challenging them to be the best in order to tap into government contracts and subsidies."

"But there are only two or three worth mentioning, right?" Doc asked. "That doesn't seem like much of a competitive field."

"Oh, there are many more big players out there, but they're staying under the radar. A high profile can put a strain on a company's resources and culture," Q commented. "They're all fierce competitors too. They have to be, in order to survive in the space industry. New technologies and the new opportunities tied to them are advancing so fast that serious competitors must take huge risks. The greater a company's goals, the greater the risks they must take. Advancements are essential and the pace is unforgiving. Companies that fall behind often have no way to recover."

Rehab was second nature to Doc. Each morning and early afternoon, he'd exercise, walk, stretch, and go for a short run. Every evening, he'd work out some more before jogging the four-mile roundtrip to the White House gate and back. He regained his strength, but he still occasionally struggled with limited movement in his left leg and hand. Doc understood that he likely would have to rely on his cane from time to time for the rest of his life. But he'd grown fond of it and passersby complimented him on it almost every day.

The Sunday following his release, Doc took Connie to a brunch at the White House as he'd promised. She was growing increasingly fond of Doc by then, and she hoped the feeling was mutual. But Doc was hard to read, so she didn't push the question. Connie had never even been to the White House as a tourist, so she was almost breathless as they were escorted to the first family's residence on the second floor. She was momentarily speechless when the President entered the room with the first lady on his arm.

"Doc! It's wonderful to see you!" the President called out from across the room. "You look fantastic. But I gotta tell ya, Doc. This young lady you have with you outshines you. Your taste for elegance and grace is very nearly as good as mine."

"But forgive me, please," the President declared. "Melanie, you know Doc. But Doc, please introduce your young lady friend."

"Hello again, Mr. President," Doc said. "Mrs. Preston, I'd like you to meet my very good friend, Ms. Connie Walters."

"I'm very pleased to meet you, Connie," the first lady stated. "I hope it's alright if I call you Connie."

"It is, absolutely, Mrs. Preston," Connie managed to say smoothly. "I'm so very pleased to actually meet you. I've admired your poise and presence from the first moment I saw you. I'm thrilled to actually meet you."

"Call me, Melanie, please," the first lady encouraged warmly. "After all, you're a guest in our home and we want our guests to feel at home too. That's a lovely dress, by the way. I just love the color."

"Oh, thank you!" Connie replied, relieved. "I so wanted to wear something appropriate. I'm glad you like it. That compliment coming from someone with your taste in clothes means a lot to me. Thank you. I may put it on an expensive hanger when I get home and just keep it as a memento of my time here."

"There's no need for that," the President specified. "We've arranged to have pictures taken of the four of us while we have you both here."

"Doc called yesterday and tipped us off that one of your favorite lunch choices is a good Reuben sandwich. And it just so happens that our chef loves a good Reuben, too. So he's prepared them in his unique way. Believe me, it's the best Reuben sandwich in the entire world."

"That sounds absolutely wonderful!" Connie confirmed with a wide grin.

Doc could tell he was batting a thousand so far. During the meal, it seemed to him that Connie and Melanie were fast becoming friends. Connie had obviously gotten over her jitters. After lunch, the four of them posed for pictures. Then Melanie gave Connie a tour of the private residence and the President led Doc into his study to talk about "the future."

"How are you really, Doc?" the President asked. "Are you as healed and healthy as you look? It was a very brave thing you did, shielding me the way you did. I'll be forever grateful, believe me. I see you have a cane with you, but I haven't seen you use it."

"I'm doing well, sir," Doc admitted. "I'm 100 percent most of the time. But every now and then, my left leg lets me know it's not happy so I always have my cane handy."

"That's a beautiful piece of work," the President congratulated. "I see you have your Trident inlaid in the handle. That's really beautifully done, Doc."

"Thank you, sir," Doc replied. "It was a gift from a very good friend."

"Well, let's get down to business," the President finally stated. "I told you while you were still in the hospital that I still have a need for your knowledge and experience, and I meant it. I've been looking for a while for the right person to fill an especially important role in my administration, and I believe you're that person. I'd greatly appreciate you accepting the appointment as my Senior Advisor for Military Affairs. Your office would be in the West Wing, just two doors down from mine. Things are heating up fast all around the globe, Doc. And I need someone with your depth of knowledge and experience to help me make the right decisions, at the right times. I can't think of anyone else's input I trust as much as I've learned to trust yours, in the short time that we worked together. You've a gift for global military affairs, Doc. Your background and training are perfectly suited for the post. You come with knowledge of the medical side of the equation as well as the tactical side. It's time you put it to the best possible use for our country. Whadaya say?"

"It's a very generous offer, Mr. President," Doc revealed hesitantly. "But it's a big decision. I'd appreciate a little time to think it through, sir. Will it be okay if I call you with my answer around this time tomorrow?"

"That'll be fine, Doc," the President replied with a smile. "Take a little longer if you need to. Think about it. Pray about it. And let me know what you decide."

A light knock on the door told the President he needed to move forward.

"Thanks for coming, Doc," he conveyed genuinely and headed out the door. "I look forward to hearing your answer. Please thank Ms. Walters for me too, good friend."

"I will," Doc insisted. "Thank you for another wonderful visit...and for the offer."

Doc told Connie about the job offer on the ride home.

"It sounds like an amazing opportunity, Doc," she expressed excitedly. "I'm so happy for you! You did accept the President's offer, didn't you?"

"No, not yet," Doc admitted slowly, staring out his side window. "I told him I'd call him with my answer tomorrow.

I guess I'll have plenty to think about on my runs this afternoon and evening."

"Plenty to think about?" Connie shot back, in exasperation. "What on earth is there to think about? You're the perfect person for the job, Doc. So it's not as though it's a reward for saving his life. You're going to take the job, aren't you?"

"I really don't know just yet, Connie," Doc acknowledged. "I know enough about the military and medicine, but you can bet there's a lot more to the job than meets the eye… not the least of which involves the unavoidable, ugly politics."

"But you can't just dismiss the opportunity of a lifetime, Doc," Connie pressed him. "Don't you owe it to yourself— and to the President—to give it your best shot? If you don't, won't you wonder about the decision for the rest of your life?"

"Perhaps," Doc murmured softly, still looking out his window. "But I'm not sure I'm cut out for a desk job just yet. I'm a 'hands-on' guy. I've always been. I've always helped carry out missions, gotten my hands dirty, and watched out for the people working with me. I made sure that jobs not only got done…but got done right. I don't see those kinds of challenges in being a desk jockey."

"A desk jockey?!" Connie almost yelled. "Is that what you think of the men and women who help the President of the United States make tough decisions that can change the world? Doc, your past jobs didn't just get your hands dirty…they almost got you killed!"

"Are we fighting?" Doc asked with a troubled look on his face.

"I'm sorry to be so upset, Doc," Connie clarified sincerely. "But your past jobs have gotten you mortally wounded more than once. Isn't that enough to move you to give up adventure?"

The two of them rode silently for the last few minutes it took to reach Connie's apartment. Doc held Connie's hand as he walked her up the steps to her front door. At the door, he kissed her lovingly. She kissed him back urgently. They hugged tightly, as snow began to fall.

"Connie, this decision isn't about moving on from the past. That decision has already been made for me. Now I've to figure out what to do with the rest of my life. And it's not just a choice between a desk job and adventure. I can sell insurance, ice cream, or time shares, if I have to. I'm just not sure that a high-profile government job will be worth the cost."

"The look on your face doesn't just worry me, Doc," Connie muttered softly. "It scares me."

"Times are scary for both of us, Connie," Doc admitted. "I wish they weren't. I hope that will change soon. But I think we should take some time and distance in the meantime."

Then Doc kissed her lovingly, hugged her close, and departed.

6

SAINT-GAUDENS' DOUBLE EAGLE

T he next day, Doc called the President to tell him he'd decided not to take the job.

"Well, I couldn't be more disappointed, Doc," the President expressed. "But I respect your decision and I wish you all the best in all you do. If there's ever anything I can do for you, just give me a call. Okay?"

"That's very kind of you, Mr. President. Thank you very much for everything," Doc contended.

"I mean it. I'm just a phone call away," the President said sincerely. "Good luck, Doc."

"Goodbye and thanks again, Mr. President," Doc conveyed and hung up.

For the next three months, Doc took a secluded, internal journey. He settled into a solitary existence in his tiny apartment above a café on the north bank of the Potomac River, in the shadow of the Francis Scott Key Memorial Bridge. Q occasionally called him, but Connie never did…

and he didn't call her. It seemed easier than trying to explain a decision she didn't understand.

Instead, he focused on regaining strength and mobility with early morning walks, late afternoon runs, and weekly rehab sessions. Whenever the hard work of healing brought Mountain to mind, Doc made calls or wrote letters in an effort to find him…with no luck. But he felt he owed it to Mountain to keep looking. It was Mountain who encouraged Doc to write the autobiography he'd finally started.

HAVING SPENT A COUPLE OF HOURS WORKING ON HIS own personal journey through life, he squirmed in his worn, squeaky office chair and stared out an open window at the Potomac. The ache in his hip had suddenly flared up and demanded his attention. Hoping for relief, he popped a pain-numbing hydrocodone tablet into his mouth and washed it down with the warm apple juice he'd poured himself when he began typing two hours earlier. He pushed his laptop aside and propped up his feet on the beat-up desk he'd bought for $40 at a resale store the week before. In the few days he'd owned the desk, he discovered that putting his feet up on it brought some relief from the pain that was steadily spreading to his back.

The sudden, stabbing pain provided an almost welcome break from the agony of struggling with words he'd promised Mountain he'd write. Doc had toyed with the idea of writing about his life for a couple of years. He knew his story could be compelling, if told in a powerful way. But the secrecy surrounding SEAL teams in general—and Warrior Teams in particular—ensured that almost no one even knew he'd served in the Navy, let alone that he was among the most decorated SEALs in the nation's history.

Rocking back in his chair, he caught a glimpse of his reflection in the mirror hanging on the wall across the room. He hadn't shaved in a week and hadn't brushed his hair that morning. If publishers could see him, dressed in badly worn jeans, and raggedy, stretched-neck tee shirt and hobbled by the relentless pain in his hip and back, they'd have a hard time believing the tales he could tell them—let alone the ones he couldn't.

Those thoughts and doubts rattled through his mind whenever he was at the keyboard, but Doc pressed forward each day, typed however much he could manage, and hoped momentum would eventually take hold and carry him to the end of the manuscript. But it didn't happen that morning. And Doc even wondered if he was writing a book worth reading. So he cradled a hot cup of coffee in his hands, rocked back in his chair, and silently wished his life was different. In that, silent, solitary moment, Doc let his guard down and self-pity struck.

What am I doing here? he thought to himself. *I worked so hard. I trained so long. I did everything my country asked of me, and more. But I never saw this coming.*

That's when his phone rang.

"Hello," greeted the caller. "Do I have the pleasure of speaking with Mr. John Holiday?"

"This is he," Doc said, tentatively.

"Mr. Holiday, this is Mr. Oliver. I represent Quest Publishing on H Street, here in D.C. I understand you're writing a book about your adventures and misadventures during your time in the military."

"How do you know that?" Doc asked with a raised eyebrow.

"Like you, Mr. Holiday, I've very reliable sources," Mr. Oliver confirmed. "I'm hoping you might be willing to meet with me at my office tomorrow to discuss your story."

"Why not," Doc said with a sigh. "It's more fun talking about it than writing about it."

"I'm glad to hear that, Mr. Holiday!" Mr. Oliver proclaimed. "Does 9:00 a.m. work for you?"

"Yep," Doc answered.

"Excellent!" Mr. Oliver suggested. "I'll send a car for you."

"Don't bother," Doc admitted. "I've seen your building. I'll enjoy the walk. Should I bring what I've written so far?"

"No need," Mr. Oliver acknowledged. "I'm familiar with your story and find it very compelling."

"But you haven't seen what I've written," Doc replied.

"Be that as it may," Mr. Oliver said, "we're prepared to make you an offer I believe you'll find very attractive."

"Well then, I'm sure I'll enjoy the walk," Doc chuckled. "I'll see you in the morning, Mr. Oliver."

"I look forward to it. Goodbye 'til then," Mr. Oliver maintained.

"Likewise," Doc said and hung up.

Doc suddenly felt energized. He walked to the window of his apartment that looked out over the Potomac below.

Until that afternoon, he'd never bothered to take in the great view from his out-of-the way, hole-in-the-wall apartment. The river was teeming with kayakers and paddleboarders enjoying a beautiful summer day on the river, set against the backdrop of the Watergate Hotel, the Kennedy Center, and the Washington Monument in the distance.

Doc finished his coffee thinking about how great it'd be if Quest Publishing gave him an advance on his book large enough to buy a small motorboat that he could cruise up and down the river in. He'd no place to store it, and no car to tow it. But at least for the moment, that was beside the point. So was the pain involved in the short walk to the kitchen to refill his coffee cup. Doc was elated by the prospect of selling his autobiography…not to mention the prospect of people reading it.

"Now all I have to do is write it," he laughed out loud as he contemplated it.

After the second cup of coffee, Doc slipped into his sweats and went for his longest jog yet. He followed the Capital Crescent to Virginia Avenue. His sweatshirt was soaked with sweat by the time he reached Maine Avenue. But he kept going. The call from Mr. Oliver was the first bright light in Doc's sullen life in months, and he was determined to use the boost it gave his spirits to push through the pain in the hope that he could eventually dispel it. Doc walked the last half mile to the National War College and sat on the grass at Greenleaf Point with his feet literally hanging in the Potomac.

Doc's body had to rest, but his thoughts kept going. He played the brief phone call over and over in his head while he rested by the water. On the long walk home, he mulled over the little information he had, but he couldn't make any sense of it. No one knew he was writing his autobiography. Few people had his cell phone number, and none knew about the book.

Predictably, Doc mulled over the call for the rest of the day and into the night until he finally fell asleep.

"What was that call really about?" he asked himself dozens of times. "And who was Mr. Oliver, truly?"

Doc was awake by 0600 and dressed by 0700 the next morning. While replaying the call repeatedly in his head the night before, he'd talked himself out of wearing a suit and tie to his meeting with Mr. Oliver. Instead, he opted for dark brown cargo pants, a black crew neck pullover, a brown heathered vest, and his Navy-issued boots. His cane slid nicely into the custom loops he'd had added to his wide leather belt and his left upper pant leg.

His back didn't hurt too much, but his left leg was stiff and sore from the workout he gave it the day before. He munched on a bagel so that he had something in his stomach when he swallowed another hydrocodone tablet. He was out the door by 0730 to give himself plenty of time for the walk up H Street, including the time he knew it'd take to get a steaming hot cup of expresso on the way.

At 0845, Doc was standing in front of the Grange Building, home of Quest Publishing. At least that's what the sign on the front of the building listed. Doc leaned against a tree, finished his expresso, and took note of the other buildings in the area. Though the block sat virtually in the shadow of the White House, it looked innocent enough. Still, with the "glow" of yesterday's phone call from Mr. Oliver dimmed significantly. Doc's instincts told him to be wary of the ease with which the supposed publisher's proposition seemed to be unfolding. His instincts were front and center as he headed into the building to meet with Mr. Oliver.

Doc followed the wall signs down a labyrinth of marble-lined hallways, deep into the building. He stood at the doorway marked Quest Publishing for a moment and listened to the silence on the other side. Doc was beginning to think that, once again, his instincts were right.

This should be interesting, Doc thought, as he opened the door and strode into the silence. Inside stood a broad, empty counter of polished wood and more marble. Upon it sat a large, shiny brass bell. The sign beside it read, "Please ring bell for service." So Doc rung it.

"Can I help you?" asked a distinguished-looking but dour older gentleman in an elegant navy blue suit as he emerged from some room or other behind the counter.

"I'm here to see Mr. Oliver," Doc offered. "I have a 9 a.m. appointment with him."

"Can you please tell me your name and what you're meeting with Mr. Oliver about?"

"I'm John Holiday," Doc said. "Mr. Oliver is interested in publishing my book."

"I see," the gentleman stated. "Please wait here. I'll be right back."

Doc's instincts were working overtime now.

"This is beyond odd," he pondered to himself as the gentleman disappeared into some room or other far behind the counter.

Out of habit or instinct, Doc rested his left hand atop the

smooth, blunt handle of his cane, like he used to do with the 45mm sidearm he carried in the SEALS. The tempered steel nerves inside of him coiled slowly as he pretended to not be paying attention while he waited. Moments later, the gentleman in navy blue reappeared. In his gloved hands, he carried an intricately carved wooden box about the size of a cigar box. He gently set it on the counter in front of Doc and gestured for him to move closer to the counter.

"I'm afraid Mr. Oliver cannot meet with you this morning, Mr. Holiday," he revealed. "But he has directed me to give you the contents of this box."

This is way, way beyond weird, now, Doc thought.

"What is it?" Doc asked innocently, ready to hold forth, with his cane if necessary.

The older gentleman lifted the ornate lid of the box and revealed a single gold coin, nested in royal blue velvet. He then pulled a pair of white cotton gloves from his jacket pocket and presented them to Doc.

"Put these on, please," he directed Doc.

"What's that?" Doc asked innocently as he slipped on the gloves.

"This is the only 1933 Saint-Gaudens Double Eagle $20 gold piece in the world in private hands. And this morning, the hands are yours," the gentleman said as he lifted the heavy, finely polished coin from its box and placed it in Doc's open right hand.

"What am I supposed to do with this?" Doc inquired, wary of the answer to come.

"Simply exit the building as you entered, turn right, and walk approximately 500 feet down H street to St. John's Episcopal Church," the gentleman told Doc. "Enter the church through the 16th Street entrance and sit on the left side of the center aisle in the sixth pew from the altar. A priest approximately my age will approach you with a velvet donation bag. When he does, extend both of your gloved hands to him palms down. Be sure to hold the coin in your left hand. He'll tap your left hand. You'll then show the priest the coin before you drop it into his donation bag. Then he'll lead you to your next step in your journey."

Doc found the scenario too mysterious to back away from at that moment, so he carefully slipped the coin into the left thigh pocket of his cargo pants and zipped it shut. The stranger left without saying goodbye and the gentleman just as quietly watched him exit the office. By this time, Doc was certain the halls were monitored by hidden cameras, which he was sure were tracing his every move on the way out of the building. His three burning questions were: Who was pulling the strings of this operation? What exactly was the mission? Were they hostile or friendly?

Back on H Street, Doc breathed a little easier and assumed "they" were friendly after Googling the $20 gold piece in his pants pocket. If it was real, Doc was walking the streets of Washington D.C. unarmed, with a coin in his pocket valued at more than $7.5 million. He figured hostile actors would never entrust him with it. His hip began to bother him, so he put his cane to use as he crossed the 500 or so feet on the way to St. John's. He stood at the corner of H and 16th streets long enough to take a good look at Lafayette Square and the north facade of the White House beyond. He thought about the President, Q, Mountain, and Connie. He wondered what each of them was doing that morning…especially Connie. He prayed he'd soon see them all again…especially Connie.

As instructed, Doc entered the church through the 16th Street entrance, despite several signs very clearly directing him to enter by way of the double doors facing H Street. Doc sat on the left side of the center aisle in the sixth pew from the altar. Within minutes, an older priest approached Doc and silently stood before him, holding a velvet donation bag open. Doc held out both of his gloved hands, palms down. As instructed, Doc held the coin in his left hand. And as expected, the priest tapped Doc's left hand. Doc then opened both hands, palms up, to show the priest the coin before he dropped it into the velvet bag. He smiled at the thought that he'd literally just let a fortune slip through his hands.

The priest silently signaled Doc to follow him and led him to the rear of the altar, and then waved him through a door that led to a small library lined with thousands of books. A pedestal stood in the center of the room with a large book laid open upon it. Alone now, Doc approached the book, flipped through its pages, and discovered a depression in the distinct shape of his Trident had been cut out of the center of roughly a hundred pages. Following his instincts again, Doc use his pocket knife to coax his Trident out of the handle of his cane. When he placed the Trident into the book's depression, a hidden door opened. He pressed the Trident back into the handle of his cane, and had to hustle through the door as it began to close. Doc now understood that he was involved in a very elaborate and well-funded enterprise of unknown origin or intent. He was still very much in the dark, but he knew a unique adventure was underway, and he wanted to see more.

In the hidden room sat two high-back chairs: one was positioned in the center of the room facing the other. They were roughly an arm's length apart. Doc settled into a chair and discovered it was a recliner.

"They've thought of everything," Doc marveled, thinking whoever his host was, he must know that reclining helped lessen the hip and back pain that plagued him. There in the perfect silence, Doc knew he'd done his part. But he'd no idea when to expect whoever would sit in the other chair. Settled in and comfortable, Doc pulled his cell phone out of one of his pockets and quickly discovered it was useless in the chamber.

Doc was piecing together what little he knew about the events unfolding in the rear of the nondescript church when a booming deep voice erupted somewhere behind him.

7

FOR THE BENEFIT OF ALL MANKIND

"I'm very happy to finally meet you, Mr. Holiday!" the voice bellowed, while Doc twisted in his chair—despite the pain it brought him—to get a look at the stranger. "And I'm thrilled that you've chosen to join me in this quest."

"I'm not sure I'm joining anything, just yet," Doc said flatly. "And who are you?"

"Names aren't vital to our success," the voice maintained. "So call me Keeper. I understand that Navy SEALs typically adopt, or are given, nicknames as soon as they begin their training. I must say, yours is extremely fitting for a trained neurosurgeon with a cowboy's knack for grand adventures…especially with the last name of Holiday."

"Well, since we're saving time on introductions, please cut right to the chase and tell me what this is all about."

"It's all very simple, really," Keeper suggested. "I need a great deal of money and I believe you're just the man who can acquire it for me while avoiding undue attention."

"I don't do anything illegal," Doc said flatly.

"I can assure you there's no need to break any laws," Keeper replied.

"Well, I'm the wrong guy to ask to co-sign a loan," Doc joked. "My FICO score sucks."

"If you succeed in this quest, I guarantee you'll never worry about your credit score again," Keeper laughed.

"That would take a lot of money," Doc asserted.

"If half of what I've recently learned is accurate, you'll have far more than a lot," Keeper insinuated.

"Money's a good place to start," Doc alleged seriously. "But it's going to take more than money to keep me here much longer."

"That's the primary reason I selected you, Mr. Holiday." Keeper sounded equally serious. "I can promise you that the vast treasure I'm after won't sit around in coffers or hedge funds. I plan to use it for the benefit of all mankind."

"Surrrrrrrre ya do," Doc acknowledged, because he'd heard that line several times too many.

"We'd like to provide you with a little context, Mr. Holiday," Keeper whispered in a softer tone. "Please sit back and watch President Preston's unveiling of the new Space Force...along with an opportunity of a lifetime."

The video appeared on an entire wall of the chamber, lending even grander weight and scale to its message.

"I'm instructing my administration to embrace the budding commercial space industry. Today, we're taking one more step to unleash the power of American ingenuity. I'm about to sign a new directive to federal departments and agencies. They'll work together with American industry to implement a state-of-the-art framework for space traffic management. Together, there's absolutely nothing Americans can't do.

"Now we're ready to begin the next great chapter of American space exploration. This is a very important day. A new generation of young people seeks to challenge—really challenge hard—to get their talent and their skill to work. And now we're giving them a forum and a platform, from which they can put that genius to work. Legions of welders and metalworkers, scientists and engineers stand ready to build powerful new rockets and gleaming new spaceships…and that goes with all the other things we're building in our country.

"Our nation of pioneers still yearn to conquer the unknown, because we are Americans and the future belongs totally to us. Once more, we'll launch intrepid souls blazing through the sky and soaring into the heavens. Once more, we will summon the American spirit to tame the next great American frontier. And once more, we proudly lead humanity beyond the earth, and into those forbidden skies. But they won't be forbidden for long. And we'll learn everything there is to know about it.

"What you're doing is so important economically, militarily, scientifically, in every way, there's no place like space."

"Doesn't that just make you want to stand up and cheer, Mr. Holiday?" Keeper asked at the end of the video. "Can you imagine all the benefits for mankind that will flow from a renewed and energized space program? And all of it will be built by private industry. But it'll take immense amounts of money for private enterprise to lead the nation in this great undertaking, to earn the President's confidence, as well as the lucrative government subsidies and contracts.

"Frankly, it's more than can be raised and committed by us separately or collectively," Keeper explained. "To make matters worse—and the challenge even greater—other corporate entities are committed to pursuing these objectives alone…to disrupt and obstruct those of us who are doing all we can to meet the President's challenge through cooperation.

"But the biggest obstacle in the way of progress is not the billions of dollars this undertaking requires now. It's the hundreds of billions it will cost into the foreseeable future.

"That, Mr. Holiday, is where you come in." Keeper finally got to the point.

"Umm, let me make sure I understand," Doc declared in disbelief. "You're telling me the President has conceived a challenge so immense that you guys don't have—and can't borrow—enough money to buy your way into the game, but it's potentially so lucrative, you won't rest until you find a way to carve out a huge piece of the action?

"So you think you have discovered some never-before-imagined way to put taxpayer money into your well-lined pockets. And here's the worst—and most amusing part—you lured me here because you think you might somehow persuade me to help you do it. Well, I hate to break this to you so bluntly, but I'm not interested."

"Of course you aren't yet, Mr. Holiday," Keeper replied. "You're no mere soldier of fortune! We knew that enlisting your help would require something of significantly more value than mere dollars and sense."

"And what could that possibly be?" Doc asked, bracing himself for another sales pitch.

"We're offering you a new lease on life, Mr. Holiday," Keeper began. "We can provide you with the best medical and rehabilitation services in the world. In fact, we've consulted the world's foremost spinal/orthopedic surgeon. We gave him a comprehensive history of your injuries, along with all the related medical records, and he's assured us there's a complete and permanent remedy for the pain you're currently living with every single day."

"How did you get all that information?" Doc asked in amazement.

"You see, Mr. Holiday, money can be used for good," Keeper reiterated with a grin. "If you agree to help us, we are prepared to cover the cost of your healing and rehabilitation. Say you'll join in our effort, and we can begin preparations to fly you to Switzerland, where you'll receive transformational surgery and state-of-the-art rehabilitation treatments that'll give you back your life. And if you then succeed at the mission we have for you, you'll never need worry about money again. Do we have a deal, Mr. Holiday?" Keeper asked.

"Not hardly," Doc replied, flatly. "You've shown me what you can do for me, but I still haven't seen what you think I can do for you."

"We need you to add your skills, knowledge, and determination to our efforts to secure an almost limitless source of funding," Keeper emphasized. "We believe a man of your qualifications and qualities working on our behalf will result in a financial reserve so large, our joint venture will be the undisputed leader in design, construction, and delivery of the powerful and efficient space vehicles and hardware our nation needs to—as the President put it so succinctly—'summon the American spirit to tame the next great American frontier.'"

"Okay, now I can see the dots," Doc admitted. "Please connect them for me."

"Have you heard of the Knights Templar, Mr. Holiday?" Keeper asked.

"Sure, they were Europe's special ops troops during the Crusades," Doc answered.

"That's exactly right," Keeper confirmed. "And they were the favorite charity of Catholics throughout Europe. They also got to keep all that they plundered throughout the Middle East. The Knights were the most powerful and wealthiest military fighting force in history. For two centuries, they accumulated such a vast treasure that even the best financial minds of our time hesitate to estimate its worth.

"But when the order was disbanded suddenly in the 14th century, no treasure was recovered, and none has been found since. Today, no governmental authority has a lawful claim to the treasure, and most experts will tell you it doesn't exist. However, a few highly respected experts concede there's a very real possibility that the Knights did have such a treasure, and took the precaution of hiding it…and that it could well exceed $400 billion in today's currency."

"Really?!" Doc inquired, partly dumbfounded and more than a little doubtful.

"Really…" Keeper stated flatly.

"What do you think?" Doc asked, even though he knew the answer.

"If I didn't think the treasure was real, we wouldn't be here discussing it, Mr. Holiday," Keeper expressed.

"And you want me to find it for you," Doc guessed.

"One final mission on behalf of the nation and all humanity," Keeper clarified.

"But why me?" Doc asked. "If you're willing to spend big money tilting at windmills, why pick a broken-down, retired sailor to help you do it? There are plenty of good men looking for a big payday."

"You're more than that, Mr. Holiday. We have your military record," Keeper highlighted.

"That's impossible," Doc insisted.

"You see, Mr. Holiday? Things thought to be impossible can be true," Keeper cautioned.

"Prove it," Doc challenged him.

"The details are safe with us, Mr. Holiday," Keeper assured him. "And we know all we need to about the sort of man you are. You are, as the Navy SEAL motto says, 'a common man with an uncommon desire to succeed.'"

"And you really believe you can put this common man back together?" Doc asked.

"Yes, I do, Mr. Holiday." Keeper locked eyes with Doc.

"You're a man of great faith," Doc noted.

"We both are, Mr. Holiday," Keeper replied. "So do we have a deal?"

Doc extended his hand to Keeper and said simply, "Call me Doc."

"And call me 'Keeper,'" Keeper proclaimed, shaking Doc's hand. "I apologize for the secrecy, Doc. But you must understand that other powerful parties are equally interested in finding the treasure…highly interested. So the more productive your efforts prove to be, the more secret they must be. With such high stakes on the line, my company, and your very life, may depend upon how little anyone else knows about who you are and what you're up to."

"So where will I look?" Doc asked.

Keeper handed Doc a narrow, sealed manila envelope.

"You'll find the details inside," he instructed, "along with a small cash advance, hotel and flight reservations, and new I.D. along with a passport and a credit card."

"You were that sure I'd accept your offer?" Doc asked with only mild surprise as he tucked the envelope safely away in the leg pocket of his cargo pants.

"Let's just say I was optimistic…and proactive." Keeper said with a grin. "You have a car waiting at the curb on 16th Street. It'll also pick you up at your place at 6:00 tomorrow morning and drive you to the airport for an early flight to Zurich. We'll have a connection waiting for you there to take you directly to the hospital. Your bags will be taken to the suite I've reserved for you. I've also opened a bank account for you there to cover expenses.

"Good luck and God be with you, Doc. I look forward to celebrating your success!"

Outside, Doc paused on the curb long enough to take

another brief look at the White House before slipping in the rear seat of the waiting Escalade. During the ride home, he opened the envelope and found his instructions, new I.D., credit card, airline ticket, passport, and $2,000 in crisp new 20s and 50s.

This is really happening, Doc thought. *I'm off to look for something almost everyone in the entire world believes doesn't exist. And most of the few who do believe it exists, want to keep me from finding it. I guess I get to put off writing my autobiography…at least until I complete this mission…which might turn out to be the most interesting chapter of all.*

He smiled and shook his head as he slipped everything back into the envelope and his ride came to a stop outside his apartment. Once he was back inside, Doc poured a glass of apple juice, popped what he hoped would be the last hydrocodone tablet into his mouth, and settled into his office chair. The trip had reawakened the pain in his hip and back, so he hoisted his feet onto his desk and rocked back as far as he could.

Doc sipped his juice and he looked out the window at the scores of people enjoying the bright afternoon sun on the Potomac. The rest of the world was oblivious to the seismic shift his life had just undergone. All he had to do was keep it that way. He pulled the manila envelope from his leg pocket and emptied the contents onto his desk. His new driver's license, credit card, and passport bore the name Jason Hightower. So did his tickets and hotel reservation. He thought his new photo was a huge improvement from the one on his real documents, so it made him smile. He thumbed through the clean, crisp cash and presumed it was real.

Doc slipped his cane from the loops that held it against his left leg and studied its polished handle, with his perfectly inlaid gold Trident. He'd come to appreciate the cane for its beauty as well as its function. And he figured he'd keep it with him however successful his upcoming surgery proved to be. That thought stirred memories of his surgeries and the days he'd spent in hospitals and rehab, which in turn sparked thoughts of Q, the President...and Connie. Doc pulled paper, envelopes, and a pen from his desk drawer and wrote each of them a short note explaining only that he'd be gone for a while and would be in touch when he returned. Then he opened his laptop, turned it on, called up the draft of his book, scrolled to where he'd left off, and smiled as he typed, "To be continued."

8

A FAIR TRADE

Doc spent his last afternoon in D.C. packing and thinking about the mission ahead. He went to bed that night contemplating the mission. His questions about it were painfully obvious and were even more painfully unanswerable.

Once I'm released from the hospital, where will this search take me? he thought. *How long will I be gone? What are the chances that there really is a treasure? What happens if I find it? What if Keeper really just wants to grab the treasure and run? What if his story about space exploration is literally just pie in the sky? What if something happens to me? Who will know? And who won't? Whatever happens, what have I got to lose?*

This train of questions recurrently looped through his sleepless brain. Doc's efforts not to think about them were like trying to stop a runaway locomotive. Somewhere around midnight, a second train of questions began dominating Doc's brain.

Who is Keeper, really? How exactly did he know so much about me, about my service record, and my injuries? How'd he get my phone number? Is he really a private businessman, or could he be with the federal government? FBI? CIA? NSA? Military Intelligence? How'd he come up with such excellently forged documentation? What if the money he gave me is as phony as my passport? How'd he arrange for my surgery? How'd he open a Swiss bank account for me? How'd he get his hands on a Saint-Gaudens Double Eagle? Was it even real? Who were the guys who steered me to him? What in the world is going on with St. John's Church? What if I'm caught with a phony passport? What have I gotten myself into?

Even as both dark, emotional trains rumbled around and around on Doc's one-track mind, he somehow managed to get a few hours of sleep. He awoke at 0500, showered, grabbed his cane and his duffle bag, and climbed into the Escalade. Ten hours later, he entered the lobby of a small hotel near Zurich's center, just a ten-minute taxi ride away from the University Hospital Zurich, where the bullet would be removed from his spine. The walk from the curb to the hotel's front desk was difficult for him after the long flight from D.C.

"I'd like a room with a king-size bed, please," he requested with a forced smile.

"Of course," the clerk said. "Could I please have your name, a photo I.D., and a credit card?"

"It's Hightower," Doc announced as he produced his license and credit card. "Jason Hightower."

"Welcome, Mr. Hightower!" the desk clerk said cheerfully. "Is this your first visit to Zurich? Did you have a good flight?"

"It is and I did!" Doc replied.

"I trust you'll find your room quite comfortable," the clerk commented, and handed Doc the room key. "Enjoy your stay!"

"I'm sure I will," Doc confirmed.

After unpacking, Doc enjoyed a light supper at a quaint restaurant just a few painful steps from the hotel. It was a challenge for him to mount the three steps that led to the front door, but the meal was wonderful. He hoped that what Keeper had promised was true. Doc clung to the reality that the mystery man had engineered and financed the events that so suddenly catapulted him from the north bank of the Potomac to the shadows of the Alps. He was scheduled to meet with the surgeon the next morning to discuss the groundbreaking surgery planned for the day after. But while he ate supper that first evening in Zurich, Doc pondered the mystery of whether he really thought Mr. Mystic's promises seemed too good to believe...or if he simply didn't know what to believe.

After dinner, Doc slowly made his way back to the hotel. He was thrilled to have a Nespresso machine waiting atop the small refrigerator in his room. He'd brought back three small pastries to enjoy with a steaming hot blend of coffee and espresso on his balcony. The railing was the perfect height for Doc to elevate his legs while he sat on a surprisingly comfortable wrought-iron chair. He set the bold, fragrant brew and three crisp-crusted walnut pastries on the table beside his chair and rested the documents from Keeper on his lap. Before he started reading, Doc took what he hoped would be the last hydrocodone tablet he'd ever need. Then he sipped the Nespresso and took a bite of pastry.

On that wonderfully mild evening under the stars, on the

east end of Zurich, Doc rested as he read the information about the contact awaiting his arrival in Rome. Her name was Madeleine Bellarose. She looked too young to have what Keeper called "an impressive and well-deserved reputation as a brilliant paleographer and a relentless researcher." She'd supposedly made a number of historic discoveries during six years of digging through long-forgotten documents in the Vatican Secret Library. Doc didn't know what a paleographer did, had no clue the Vatican had a secret library, and was unsure of what it contained, but he knew Madeleine Bellarose was beautiful. So he was eager to meet her, whether or not she had any useful information about the so-called lost treasure of the Knights Templar.

As Doc studied the material from Keeper, the pain in his hip and back worsened to the point of distraction. He used the railing to pull himself to his feet and did some stretching exercises, but they didn't help that night. Hoping for some relief, Doc grabbed a pillow from his bed, wedged it behind him on the balcony chair, and again propped his feet atop the railing. Again, it didn't help. When squirming brought no relief, Doc neatly stacked the papers on the dresser, retreated to the bed, and stretched out beneath the covers. He knew that even if sleep didn't come, he at least needed to rest before dawn arrived. A short time later, the hydrocodone did its work and sleep silently slipped into bed with Doc. So he was reasonably rested when the alarm of his watch went off. He quickly showered, shaved, and had the hotel summon a taxi for the short ride to his appointment.

Doc braced himself for a drawn out process, requiring a long wait before the surgeon finally appeared for a two- or three-minute conversation with him about what the next day's surgery would be like. But shortly after Doc arrived at the hospital, the surgeon appeared.

"How do you do, Mr. Hightower," the surgeon greeted with a broad smile. "I'm Doctor Schmid. I'm pleased to meet you—and equally pleased that I fully expect to be able to completely relieve your pain once and for all."

"Pleased to meet you too, doctor," Doc expressed. "But I hope you understand when I say your confidence and assurance sound too good to be true. I've consulted a number of experts in America, who all cautioned that removing the fragment from my spine was too risky a procedure."

"Yes, I was informed of that," the surgeon replied. "But I've devised a procedure that has proven to be most effective in dozens of cases like yours. I've successfully removed fragments—and in one case an entire bullet—with no complications and completely restored patients' range of motion without pain. How does that sound to you, Mr. Hightower?"

"Well, as we say in America, Doctor," Doc alleged, "I'm from Missouri. Show me."

"Where's Missouri, Mr. Hightower?" the surgeon asked innocently.

"Smack dab in the heart of our country," Doc chuckled. "Where it belongs."

"You'll need to arrive by 6:00 tomorrow morning," the doctor instructed. "The surgery will begin at 7:00 o'clock. Assuming all goes well, the bullet fragment—and your pain —will be gone by 8:00 o'clock. This time tomorrow, you'll be a new man, Mr. Hightower."

"Sounds wonderful, Doctor," Doc stated with a smile. "But like I said, I'm from Missouri."

"I shall show you, Mr. Hightower," the surgeon chuckled. "But for now, I suggest that you return to your hotel and completely relax until tomorrow morning. There's no need to aggravate your condition now that you're close to bidding it farewell."

"Finally," Doc sighed, "a doctor's order I can live with. See you tomorrow, Doctor."

"I look forward to it, Mr. Hightower," the doctor muttered and left the exam room.

When Doc returned to his hotel room, he'd a strong sense that someone had been there while he was gone. Nothing looked out of place. But a vibe in the room triggered Doc's well-tuned sixth sense and he was certain someone had been there. At first, Doc wasn't concerned because he'd taken everything of value, including his passport, with him to his appointment. But then, he saw the information Keeper had given to him concerning Madeleine Bellarose. Doc was sure he'd left the pages in a perfectly neat stack on the dresser. Now, he was equally sure someone had shuffled through them and set them back on the dresser a little too casually, so he called the front desk.

"Hello, this is Mr. Hightower," he identified. "I've been gone all morning, but I'm wondering if anyone came to the hotel looking for me while I was gone."

"No sir, Mr. Hightower," the desk clerk replied. "Visitors are always noted in writing here at the desk. There have been no visitors for you since your arrival."

"Thank you very much," Doc added and hung up.

For the next 20 or 30 minutes, he tried to convince himself he might be imagining things, but his obsessive habit of arranging paper in perfectly neat stacks wouldn't let his brain settle. He returned to the dresser for another look at the stack. It'd definitely been disturbed. His next thought was that perhaps leaving the door wall to the patio open was the answer? He'd left it open just enough to allow fresh air into his room. Being on the top floor, it seemed like a safe enough move. Maybe the wind had picked up during the morning and blown the papers just enough to disturb the stack? That's when Doc noticed the second clue. He'd left the door wall halfway open. Now it was barely a quarter of the way open. Any wind strong enough to move the glass doors would have blown the papers completely off the dresser, but it hadn't.

Doc remembered the security camera in the hallway and headed down to the desk.

"Hi, I called down here a little bit ago asking whether I'd had a visitor while I was gone this morning," he told the desk clerk.

"Yes, Mr. Hightower," the clerk confirmed. "I can assure you visitors would have been noted here at the desk, and none was."

"Can we review your videotape for the seventh floor?" Doc asked.

"Certainly," the clerk verified. "We can do that right here at the desk. Come around."

The clerk hit "rewind," then "fast-forward," and they watched the tape together. It took only a minute or so, and they saw only Doc exit and re-enter his room.

"Hmmm," Doc remarked, satisfied that no one slipped past the front desk unseen.

But Doc couldn't deny what he knew. The paperwork had definitely been disturbed. He returned to the seventh floor and parked himself on the balcony with another cup of Nespresso. The puzzle was clear. He'd had a visitor that morning, but no one passed through his door. That only left the door wall, which Doc was also sure had been disturbed. The rooms on either side of his had no balcony, so his visitor had to have come from below. Doc's room was at the front of the hotel, visible from the busy street below. The room beneath his had no balcony. It didn't make sense that someone climbed to his balcony all the way from the busy street in front of the hotel. Then Doc looked up at the overhang above him.

"Could someone have come from the roof?" he wondered, and moved his chair over a bit.

Standing on the chair gave Doc just enough height to survey the low-sloping roof. The bright afternoon sun shone on the shingles and revealed footprints left by someone who walked from the peak to where Doc stood on the chair. So he quickly pulled the table over, stacked the chair on top of it, and ignored the surgeon's directive to relax the rest of the day. Instead, Doc climbed onto the roof and walked to the peak, where he was not surprised to see the trail of footprints continue to the edge of the roof at the rear of the building. Doc spotted a small grappling hook imbedded in the roof beside the path, about three feet from the edge.

Doc recognized the hook as the type used in SEAL grappling guns. It had a remote cable release, so the cable went with whoever used it, making for a clean escape to inexperienced eyes. But for Doc, the hook was an unmistakable calling card…left by a brother in arms. Judging by the size of the footprints, he was well over six feet tall. Knowing what it took to quickly and silently scale the seven-story building and leave undetected, Doc was sure the intruder was quite strong. Whoever it was got a good look at the information Doc received from Keeper—and probably took pictures of the pages. Aside from that, Doc couldn't be sure just how much his opponent knew about the hunt or about the potential size of the treasure and where to look. Was he foreign or American? Another well-financed hired gun, or a lone wolf?

What Doc did know was that he had a worthy opponent: someone big, strong, resourceful, and cunning. Nevertheless, Doc was confident his rival had gained no advantage, because Doc had taken the precaution of putting the packet's cover page in his shirt pocket the night before. So the intruder didn't have Madeleine Bellarose's name, photo, contact info, or the critical fact that she worked in the Vatican's Secret Library. The rival had learned Doc was headed to Rome. But in the process, he revealed his existence. That seemed like a fair trade.

Almost as an afterthought, Doc wondered what the intruder would've done if he'd found Doc in the room when he came off the roof. Would he have fled, or fought to the death? Doc saw no point in worrying about it until they finally met—and he was sure they would. In that moment, he figured the culprit might already be headed to Rome. But just to be on the safe side that night, he locked the door wall and moved the bed against it before going to sleep.

9

FINDING NOAH...AND HEMA

Doc awoke before dawn the next morning, ready for the new lease on life Dr. Schmid had promised him. He showered, shaved, dressed, and had the desk call for a taxi. Doc arrived at the hospital a half hour early. Less than an hour later, he was counting backward from 100 and lost consciousness at 93. When Doc awoke in the recovery room, he was thrilled to only feel the relatively minor discomfort of the incision made by the surgeon.

Doc was pain-free and ready for action! Amazed and thrilled to feel like his old self, Doc sat up and swung his legs off the bed, eager to stand without pain in his hip and back. Two nearby nurses scrambled to keep him in bed, but failed.

"Call Dr. Schmid!" one yelled to the Nurses' Station just outside the Recovery Room.

"Tell him I said thanks!" Doc yelled in the direction of the door. "I've got work to do!"

"Doctor's orders are for you to rest today and undergo at least two days of therapy before you're released," one of the nurses told him.

"Sorry, but I really can't stay," Doc answered and bolted toward the hallway. "Tell the doctor I feel terrific, and I'll send him something special from Rome."

Still a little dizzy from the anesthesia, Doc wobbled down the hallway, but made it to the elevator and reached his room by the time Dr. Schmid caught up with him.

"I really cannot release you in good conscience, Mr. Hightower," the surgeon professed.

"But you can't force me to stay either, right?" Doc replied, pulling his clothes on.

"That's correct, but it's really not advisable for you to leave before we at least know your incision is healing nicely," the surgeon explained.

"I've taken care of many incisions, doc," Doc assured the surgeon. "I'll be just fine. You did a wonderful job; I can feel it! Or should I say, I can't feel it!" Doc praised triumphantly.

Fully dressed, Doc stepped up to the Nurses' Station, where a nurse handed him a release to sign along with a plastic bag containing his cash and watch.

"Since you're intent on leaving, I wish you luck Mr. Hightower," she suggested and flashed him her best smile.

"I appreciate that very much," he said, smiling back.

Doc put the bag under one arm and headed out of the hospital. He hailed a taxi and picked up his duffle bag at the hotel 20 minutes later, then headed to the airport to catch the next flight to Rome. On the way, he chuckled quietly to himself about the fuss the hospital staff made regarding the minor discomfort of his incision. The truth was he felt great!

Doc made a point of using his cane at the airport so that security wouldn't give him a hard time about taking it onto the plane. He bought a ticket at the gate and took a seat to wait for his plane to pull up to the concourse. While he waited, a young, fresh-faced marine caught sight of the gold Trident inlaid in the handle of Doc's cane and came to an abrupt halt directly in front of Doc, snapped to attention, and gave him a crisp, perfect salute. Doc rose to his feet, made eye contact, and returned the salute.

"Semper Fi, Corporal," Doc announced softly but firmly.

"Thank you for your service, sir," the marine said quietly, and was quickly gone.

Doc missed his time in the military. He was deeply grateful for the purpose and direction it provided, and the opportunities it gave him to be of service to the nation. He'd be forever grateful for the appreciation and respect that he and others in the military shared for one another.

The brief, but momentous, encounter snapped Doc's mind back into Warrior mode. It made no sense for him to run from some unknown person hiding in the shadows. It was critical for Doc to flush out his adversary—and to do it sooner, rather than later. But it would be next to impossible to do it onboard an airplane. Doc had to throw his opponent a curve ball.

He doesn't know my next move, Doc thought. *The information he saw told him I was headed to Rome. But without the cover page, he has no idea how or when I'll get there. Unsure of my plan, he's got to be nearby, so close I could grab him—if only I knew who he was.*

Doc looked around at the other passengers waiting to board the flight.

He's got to be here right now, Doc thought.

Doc wound up and threw the best curve ball he could think of. He double-timed it out of the airport, grabbed a taxi out front, and headed to the train station. Doc spent the short ride trying to spot another taxi following his. If there was one, he couldn't see it. But the streets were crowded, so he couldn't be sure. But Doc was at least certain that he'd have more opportunities—and seven and a half hours—to identify his adversary on the train. At the station, he bought a coach seat so he could move about freely onboard. He figured the more chances he had to see who else was on board, the more likely it was that he'd eventually identify whoever was following him.

Doc was among the first to board the train. He picked a window seat and quickly hunkered down for a nap. He was tired and there'd be time enough for a good game of cat and mouse once he was more awake. Besides, he wanted to give the mystery passenger time to settle in, so he'd be caught off guard when Doc moved to another car. Satisfied that he'd set an effective trap, Doc slid his cane through the loops on his belt and pant leg, reclined his seat, closed his heavy eyelids, and fell asleep almost immediately.

A little more than two hours later, Doc awoke surrounded by the breathtaking majesty of the Swiss Alps. The immensity of God's incredible work filling his window was reason enough to be thankful he'd taken the train.

"Aren't they beautiful?" a deep, resonate voice said softly beside him.

Doc had been so distracted by the view, he hadn't given any thought to whether someone had sat beside him. He turned his head and took in the sight of a tall, powerfully built, young black man who was almost too big for his seat. Doc steadied himself for whatever came next.

Is this my mystery man? his mind asked as he sorted through the puzzle pieces set before him. *No way. He's too young. But maybe that's his cover? If so, there's no reason for him to show himself so soon. He'd be blowing his cover. He must know I'm not about to simply lead him to my Rome contact. But perhaps he's just too inexperienced or not clever enough for this business?*

Doc's analysis released the pressure in mere seconds. He realized the man beside him was either a friendly fellow traveler, or a terribly unworthy opponent.

"Yes," Doc replied, locking eyes with the young man. "Incredibly so. It's my first time seeing them. Have you made this trip before?"

"Many times," the young man replied. "But they never fail to amaze me. Every season, every sort of weather, and any time of day casts them in ways too beautiful to ever be unexciting."

If this is him, he's remarkably calm, Doc quickly and silently reasoned. *So he's either experienced far beyond his years—which could make him very dangerous. Or he's just too young to understand the danger I represent—which means I have nothing to fear.*

"As you've probably guessed, I'm American," Doc announced. "And Americans always begin conversations the same way. I'm Jason Hightower and I'm pleased to meet you. What's your name and what do you do for a living?"

"I'm pleased to meet you too, Mr. Hightower," the young man replied with an easy smile. "I'm Noah Allaman. I'm a Swiss student at the Florence School of Stadium Architecture."

"But this train goes to Rome," Doc replied.

"Yes, it does," Noah said. "That's where my true passion lies. I'm serving as a HEMA instructor there for the summer."

"What's HEMA?" Doc asked without a clue.

"Historic European Martial Arts," Noah said excitedly. "You've never heard of it?"

"I don't believe anyone has," Doc suggested matter-of-factly.

"That's not true," Noah shot back. "HEMA's taught and practiced around the world."

"Sword fighting?" Doc inquired almost dismissively.

"Sort of," Noah laughed. "But it's more about hand-to-hand combat, often with multiple opponents, using longswords, estocs, battle axes, daggers, and other weapons."

"Really?!" Doc asked with fresh interest. "You mean men still do that?"

"Men and women," Noah told him. "It's growing in popularity among people from all walks of life because it blends strength and flexibility training with myth and our modern day, romantic notions of chivalry and honor. In an age of 'anything goes,' it gives people the much-needed assurance that chivalry, bravery, honor, and glory haven't died after all."

"If HEMA can do all that, sign me up!" Doc confessed almost offhandedly.

"I'd love to," Noah said seriously. "I'd be happy to introduce you to it while you're in Rome. And when you return to America, you'll find a growing number of schools. I understand there's quite an excellent one in Atlanta for instance, wherever that is."

They both laughed and felt a friendship beginning.

"Seriously, Noah," Doc revealed. "I've just undergone surgery to correct a debilitating injury that sidelined me for quite a while. On top of that, I was wounded a number of times in the service. My range of motion is improving, but my flexibility still sucks. I could really use a good regimen of strength and flexibility training. And I would love learning new…I mean old…hand-to-hand combat techniques."

"How long will you be in Rome?" Noah asked.

"I'm sure yet," Doc stated honestly. "I'm meeting someone there as part of an assignment I'm on, and I'm not at all sure how long it will take to learn all I need to know. But while I'm there, I'd love some lessons."

"That's fantastic!" Noah said loudly as he and Doc fistbumped. "Praise God! You want to hear something amazing?"

"Amaze me some more, Noah," Doc suggested with a smile.

"I always make a point of getting a window seat," Noah explained. "But I was delayed today and when I finally got to the train, I was disappointed to find them all taken. And then—it took me so long to walk through all the other cars, this was the only seat left by the time I got to this last car. I was disappointed not to get a window seat. But then I thought, 'Noah, do you really believe everything happens for a reason, or don't you?' Then I sat my butt down next to you. And it just so happens that you badly need precisely what I have to offer you," Noah said with a bright broad smile and a heartwarming laugh. "The Lord truly does work in mysterious ways!"

"Amen!" Doc rejoiced with a laugh. "You can say that again, brother."

Neither man yet knew how well-founded their trust in God's ways truly was.

10

A PERFECT STORM

D oc was eager to learn all he could about his new friend…and HEMA. So he put thoughts of his hidden adversary on hold for a while longer. There'd be time enough before the train reached Rome. For the moment, Doc was more interested in this unexpected opportunity to begin restoring himself to his former battle-ready condition. It wasn't as though recent events had yet convinced him danger was in the air. But he had begun allowing for the possibility that it could be. And if his unseen rival resorted to violence, Doc's plan was to be ready for it.

"So, you're Swiss?" Doc asked Noah. "You sound almost American."

"I'm sorta both," Noah answered with a smile. "My parents moved to Zurich from New York when I was ten. They're Roman Catholic missionaries and have evangelized in the Valais, literally in the shadow of the Matterhorn for nearly ten years now."

"A millennial, black, Roman Catholic, Swiss, New Yorker who teaches historic European martial arts, now I can honestly say I've heard of everything," Doc commented with a belly laugh.

"With God, all things are possible!" Noah laughed along with him.

"So what brings you to Italy, Mr. Hightower, and why Rome?" Noah asked.

"I'm going to work with a contact in Rome on sort of a history project of my own," Doc told him as much as he felt he could.

"Really?" Noah inquired. "What sort of history?"

"Well, I guess you could say I'm determined to find out how accurate stories are about the Knights Templar," Doc suggested with a shrug.

"Why the Templars, Mr. Hightower?" Noah asked with heightened interest.

"You could say I've been tasked by a client to find out how much about them is true...and how much is myth. I've been directed to an expert in Rome to help me learn what I can."

"My gosh!" Noah almost shouted. "How interesting!"

"Ya think so?" Doc asked, half-serious, half-suspicious.

Doc was deadlocked between contradictory possibilities. Either this young stranger just happened to sit next to him and was innocently interested in the Knights Templar...or else he deliberately sat next to him because he was the adversary who scaled a Zurich hotel in search of clues to the huge fortune the Templars supposedly lost? Doc needed to know which it was, so he continued the conversation to see where it would lead.

"Personally, I don't know much about them," Doc sighed. "How about you?"

"Are you kidding?!" the young man asked with wide eyes. "I doubt HEMA would exist without the Templars!"

"What do you mean?" Doc asked.

"They were the elite fighting force of their time," Noah advised. "Created in 1911 by Pope Callixtus II as a military order of monks, its members were told they were 'The Mighty Hand of God,' sent forth to protect Christian pilgrims traveling between Europe and the Holy Land. Perhaps unknowingly, perhaps not, the Catholic Church set a perfect storm in motion by sanctioning and rewarding the first true Christian soldiers, who became the most prolific and lethal warriors on the face of the earth for the next 200 years. Their legendary hand-to-hand combat moves compelled armies all across Europe and the Middle East to improve, and are therefore responsible for HEMA's credibility and popularity to this day."

"Did you get those muscles waving swords around?" Doc asked somewhat innocently.

"It's much, much more than waving swords around, Mr. Hightower," Noah chuckled. "A 14th century longsword could weigh as much as 30 pounds. Add armor weighing 50 pounds or more and you get some idea why knights needed amazing strength and endurance just to survive a battle. Some of our best HEMA practitioners are also Olympic powerlifters who found HEMA while searching for ways to add grace and speed to their lifts."

"Really?!" Doc asked with rapidly growing interest. "Listen, Noah," he acknowledged. "I'm deeply serious about finding my way back to the health and strength I used to enjoy. I'd really appreciate it if you'll show me some of the basics when we get to Rome. I'll make it worth your while; and if it works I'll be forever in your debt."

Noah had noticed Doc's cane, with its inlaid SEAL Trident, early in their conversation.

"You must have once been in the greatest possible shape, Mr. Hightower," Noah indicated, giving the cane another look, then meeting Doc's gaze. "I'd be honored to help get you back in the shape America once called you to."

"Now you're talkin', Noah!" Doc said, fist-bumping the young man again.

Doc now believed Noah was who he said he was.

"By the way," he remarked as the seal of their new friendship. "Just call me Doc."

"Are you a doctor?" Noah asked.

"In another life," Doc said with a momentary far-off look. "In another life."

"I'd like to hear about that sometime, Doc," Noah suggested earnestly.

"Oh, I'm sure you and I have much to talk about," Doc replied with a smile.

Doc finally turned his attention toward his more immediate need: identifying his hidden adversary who, if Doc's instincts were still worth anything, had to be aboard the train.

"Now, if you'll excuse me, I have to stretch my legs," Doc announced and scooted past Noah.

As Doc walked the aisles of the next several rail cars, he lightly tapped his cane on the floor with every other stride. As he strolled, he turned his familiar phrase over and over in his head.

I have a good reason to know who my rival is, he thought to himself. *So why is nothing happening?*

The thought reminded Doc of something Thunder Two once told him: "If nothing's happening, you can be sure God has his reasons. Every now and again, one of his reasons may also be one of your reasons. But whatever happens, you can be sure nothing just happens."

Doc missed Thunder Two and the rest of the SEAL Team Warriors. He made a silent pledge to reach out to every member once this mission was complete, and to make a greater effort to find Mountain, who'd been incommunicado since the Oman mission. Doc lightly tapped the handle of his cane to his head to drive home his pledge. Then he playfully twirled it in his fingers like a baton. Still needing practice with the maneuver, he almost lost control of it and had to quickly capture it in his other hand. It was an impressive reflexive move, but Doc still hoped no one in the crowded car saw it. As he scanned the crowd to check, he caught the rear view of a very large man, who had bolted from his seat at the far end of the car, and was headed to the next car.

Hmm, Doc wondered. *That's a very big guy. Is he just in a hurry to get to another car, or is he dodging me?*

Doc decided to follow him and see. He quickly moved to the rear of the car and caught a glimpse of the tall passenger, who was already exiting the next car at the far end. Doc jogged through the next car and hurriedly entered the one behind it. By then, the roving passenger had already exited the next car and was hustling through the car behind it.

He's moving way too fast for an innocent explanation, Doc deduced and broke into an all-out sprint in an effort to catch up with his target. Doc raced through the next two cars, deftly dodging and sidestepping other passengers in the aisleway as he went. And all along the way, he was grateful for Dr. Schmid's miracle surgery…and for God's miracle of bringing the two of them together. As Doc raced into the last car, he saw only calm, serene passengers quietly talking to one another, or staring at the passing scenery, or sleeping. The massive runner was nowhere in sight. To be sure, Doc slowly moved along the aisle one row of seats at a time, making sure the runner wasn't slumped down to blend in. He wasn't.

Where'd he go? Doc silently wondered.

Then he thought of the big guy's rooftop move in Zurich. Doc stepped onto the platform outside the far end of the last car and discovered it was ringed by a wrought iron railing just high enough to make it relatively easy to climb onto the car's roof, especially for an experienced roof climber. Feeling more and more like the Doc of old, the newly-minted Doc moved deftly onto the railing and peered up, onto the roof of the car. He could see his target carefully moving past the high-voltage electrical technology that propelled the train along the track at more than 80 kilometers an hour. His gut told him to initiate a chase, but his logic prevailed. As good as Doc felt, he knew he wasn't up to the strength and agility it would require.

Besides, he wisely concluded to himself, *where's he going to go that I can't walk to inside the train...unless, of course, he plans to ride on top of the train the rest of the way to Rome. If he's that nuts, and desperate not to be caught, I sure don't want to be on the roof of a moving train with him.*

Before climbing back down to the car's platform, he took one last look at what he could see of the stranger.

He's awfully big alright, Doc thought, *and strong, and fearless...or just plain crazy.*

Doc felt a slight shiver as his mind raced past the briefest glimpse of a thought that the stranger reminded him of Mountain.

But there's no way it could be him, Doc argued with a shiver. *His hip was shattered into toothpick-size pieces in at least one spot. I saw the x-ray myself. And he nearly bled to death before we got him to the ship. There's just no way he could be climbing around like that.*

Doc stepped back into the rear car and headed forward at a fast clip. He hoped he might catch the stranger before he was able to scramble down from the roof and blend back in among the passengers in one of the more crowded cars. But he had no such luck. When he returned to his seat, Noah was sitting in it.

"I didn't think you'd mind," he suggested with an impish grin.

"Consider it an even trade for my first HEMA session," Doc said with a grin and settled into the aisle seat.

"You got it!" Noah replied happily. "Did you enjoy your walk?"

"Let's just say I found it beneficial," Doc answered.

Noah's question set Doc's thoughts back to the distant sight of the huge stranger scrambling quickly across the roof of the train, despite the very real danger of high-voltage electrical equipment, not to mention the speed and rocking of the train.

How many men can there be with that much moxie, who are also as big as Mountain? his mind asked.

But as far as Doc was concerned, size, strength, and courage were only half the equation. Doc couldn't imagine Mountain working against him this way.

There's no way! Doc argued with himself. *He'd never join an opposing team, not for all the tea in China...or even for all the loot in the lost treasure of the Knights Templar.*

But Doc suddenly had to admit that the last part of his argument made him pause.

Keeper waved more than $400 billion in front of me to get me to sign on, Doc recalled. *Who knows what someone might have waved in front of Mountain? Or maybe Mountain somehow learned of my mission and figured he'd muscle his way into the whole $400 billion, instead of settling for a measly percentage, like I did?*

Doc settled himself down with the reminder that it was mere speculation until he knew more. And now that he'd achieved at least a glimpse of the stranger, he was willing to wait until they reached Rome in a couple more hours to give him any more thought.

He now knows I'm on to him, Doc reasoned with himself. *So he's going to be more careful following me to Ms. Bellarose. But knowing what I now know about him, I might be best served by focusing on giving him the slip and getting to the Secret Library without him on my tail.*

"So where were we?" Doc joyfully asked Noah. "Tell me more about why some Olympic powerlifters include HEMA training in their regimens."

"HEMA requires smooth and powerful full body movements," Noah told him, "so it translates very closely with the skills required in powerlifting. For instance, the lunge in sword fighting is very similar to the movement required for a successful clean and jerk in powerlifting. The move in either sport feels completely familiar to the other. Exploding from low stances and working in low stances in general absolutely requires very similar explosive power in both sports."

"Well, powerlifting certainly explains your physique," Doc noted. "And you're saying that most HEMA athletes powerlift?"

"The serious ones, yes," Noah said.

"So, we'll be lifting?" Doc questioned.

"If you're up for it, absolutely," Noah replied. "I couldn't perform at the level I do without incorporating powerlifting into my workouts. My body simply wouldn't hold up. Thanks to the added muscle mass protecting my bones and joints, I'm virtually injury-free after several years of full contact with steel swords and fighting in taxing postures that strain the body."

"How much muscle mass would you say you've lost since leaving the SEALs?" Noah asked in making his point. "You've no doubt lost flexibility and range of movement too. If you're serious about this, I believe I can help you recoup most, if not all of it, despite your age."

"Are you saying I'm old?" Doc asked in mock protest.

"Older, not old," Noah quickly clarified. "Training strategically, I believe you will be amazed at how much of your peak performance you will reclaim."

"Well, I gotta tell ya, young fella," Doc confessed while rubbing his hands together, "I'm normally a very tough sell. But you got me buying into this. When do we start?"

"I'll be at the training center tomorrow afternoon," Noah remarked and handed Doc a card with the address and a phone number.

"I've got to meet with my contact mid-morning," Doc thought out loud. "That will likely take a couple hours. How about if we meet around 3 p.m.?"

"Sounds perfect," Noah answered. "Now, if you don't mind, I've got some reading to do for an architecture class I took an incomplete in this past semester. I promised my father I'd do it."

"Absolutely!" Doc replied, and settled back for another nap.

Just minutes before the train pulled into the Roma Termini, Doc awoke and stretched as Noah completed his reading.

"We're men with similar timing, but vastly different disciplines," Doc laughed.

"Tomorrow at 3 p.m., that changes forever," Noah proclaimed with a big smile.

11

THE VATICAN'S SECRET ARCHIVES

D oc and Noah both rose to their feet as the train came to a full stop.

"I've friends picking me up in a car," Noah maintained. "Can we give you a lift somewhere?"

"No thanks," Doc replied. "My hotel's not that far, and I'm sure I'll enjoy the walk."

"Okay," Noah revealed. "See you tomorrow at 3 p.m."

"I'm looking forward to it," Doc confirmed and headed for the exit.

As Doc crossed the platform, he surveyed the swarm of exiting passengers as casually as he could in the hope of spotting the tall stranger. But he didn't see him. Doc refused to think about the stranger during the walk to his hotel. The day was perfect. The route was beautiful. Doc wished the 20-minute walk to his hotel had been a bit longer. The upside was that he knew he had a note from Ms. Madeleine Bellarose waiting for him there. It'd contain his instructions for their rendezvous, set to happen the next day. Doc was looking forward to meeting her. In the small picture he had of her, she looked to be a dark, French beauty, with shoulder-length auburn hair and powerful brown eyes. Having not seen, or even spoken with, Connie for months, he was ready for some beauty in his life, even for purely business reasons.

The ornately carved front desk of the tiny Hotel Leone was impressive. Its lacquered finish made the dark wood gleam in the soft lights of the lobby. The desk was a heavy, roughly chiseled plank resting on the heads of two seated lions.

"Good evening!" Doc greeted happily as he approached the desk. "I'm Mr. Jason Hightower. I have a room reserved for the week."

"Buona serata, Mr. Hightower!" the desk clerk cheerfully replied. "We're pleased you've chosen to stay with us. Do you have any bags?"

"Just this one at my feet. I travel quite light," Doc indicated.

"Eccellente!" the desk clerk said, and handed Doc a gold key on a silver lion fob. "Room 7 is ready and waiting for you. I trust you'll find it quite comfortable, Mr. Hightower."

"I'm sure I will, thank you," Doc replied.

"Oh, and you have a note," the clerk suggested and handed it to Doc.

"Grazie! Thank you very much. Buona serata!" Doc remarked and headed to his room.

"Prego, Mr. Hightower!" the clerk chimed back.

Doc's room was on the ground floor and quite cozy. There was no balcony this time, but that hardly mattered. Doc was pretty sure the stranger would never be far away from him in Rome. So there was no need to worry that the stranger would try to get in the room when Doc was away. There was a large window and Doc opened it wide to enjoy the breeze while he made himself comfortable on the queen-size bed and read Ms. Bellarose's note.

Dear Mr. Hightower, it began.

It appeared that she didn't know his real name.

I'm looking forward to introducing you to some of the more interesting and important information I've recently come upon in the Papal Secret Library. I'm confident you'll agree that it was worth the time, money, and effort required to travel here from the U.S.

I'll await your arrival for lunch at noon tomorrow in the Old Bridge Gelateria, at Viale dei Bastioni di Michelangelo, #5. Come join me for the most wonderful gelato in Rome. Don't worry if you don't have a favorite flavor, because I've tried them all and won't steer you wrong! I'll set my purse on the table, so you'll know where I'm sitting. See you then!

Doc guessed she didn't know he had her photo. He could easily pick her out in any crowded room. He thought her note sounded more American than French, but he couldn't have cared less. A French accent might have just made him more nervous around her, anyway. But that was a day away. At the moment, Doc was ready for supper and slipped into Antico Forno Roscioli, the bread and pizza bakery just a few steps down the block from the hotel. The smells drifting from it made Doc's mouth water when he first entered the hotel. The place didn't need word-of-mouth endorsements; the fragrant breeze was enough to keep the joint crowded.

"Wow!" Doc uttered out loud with his first bite of the heavenly pizza. "The first slice was gone almost immediately."

"You like the pizza?" a patron at the next table asked him.

"Delizioso!" Doc bellowed and rocked back in his chair to rub his stomach. "Far better than America's best! I don't know what took me so long to visit Rome!"

Everyone at the tables surrounding Doc laughed at his enthusiasm for his meal. He always kept a low profile on missions, but this was a rare moment—an evening of relaxation in a beautiful city, with nowhere to go until his lunch date with a gorgeous woman the next day. He expected that Ms. Bellarose would be eager to meet with him and that she might talk for hours about the information she had concerning the Knights Templar and their so-called lost treasure.

After another savory bite of pizza, Doc took a long sip of his Chianti. This was life at its best for a lone, seasoned, and tested warrior, resting and learning to love days without battles. The night was young, but Doc planned to turn in early. He looked forward to a good and long night's sleep before rising in the morning to prepare for his meeting with his beautiful contact. Doc slouched in his chair, stretched out his legs, and polished off his pizza and Chianti. As solitary as it was, the night was perfect in its simplicity. Even thoughts of his shy shadow couldn't complicate it. Although it seemed the dark character was never far off, he appeared to be more interested in where Doc might be going than the foe was in knowing where

Doc was at any given moment. And in that serene moment, Doc didn't care if the stranger lurked nearby or was a million miles away.

After supper, Doc showered, set the alarm on his watch, and found some soothing music on the clock radio beside the bed. He was surprised to be as tired as he was at such an early hour. But then, he'd been on the move since leaving D.C., scrambling across a rooftop, and running through an entire moving train full of passengers. In between, he'd stumbled upon the art and science of Historic European Martial Arts and befriended an instructor who offered to help him restore his strength and flexibility. Doc had indeed been busy. So that early evening in Rome, just hours from a meeting that could conceivably launch him on a multi-billion dollar quest, he happily turned out the bedside lamp and immediately went to sleep.

The next morning, Doc awoke early, threw on sweats and running shoes, and went for a brisk walk to greet the dawn. The day ahead appeared interesting and exciting. That fact alone put a spring in Doc's step. The more steps he took, the faster he moved, and the more certain he was that the day would be at least as interesting and rewarding as he imagined. Doc broke into a full run two blocks from the River Tiber, touched the low retaining wall alongside it, and ran all the way back to the hotel. He arrived winded and wobbly, but he was deeply grateful to have accomplished a feat he would have thought impossible just two weeks earlier. He quickly stripped off his soaked sweats and jumped into a long, hot shower. His muscles needed it, and his schedule allowed it.

"Ms. Bellarose, here I come!" Doc proclaimed out loud as

he pulled on a clean sport shirt and jeans, sprayed on some after shave, and headed to the Old Bridge Gelateria.

The Old Bridge was literally steps from the Vatican. He saw Madeleine Bellarose the moment he set foot inside the door. She was impossible to miss, especially since he'd spent time with her photograph every day since he received it from Keeper.

"Ciao, Ms. Bellarose!" Doc exclaimed before he even reached her table.

"Ciao, Mr. Hightower," she replied.

"Call me, Jason, please," he asked of her. "I see you've ordered already."

"Oh, yes," she agreed. "The gelato here is the best in Rome, maybe all of Italy? I don't often stop for lunch when I'm working. So today was a wonderful excuse to come here and indulge myself. Everything here is wonderful. But it seems I always end up with my favorite: Ricotta Pistachio."

"I'm partial to chocolate," Doc confessed, staring through the glass at the dozens of flavors.

"Then you simply must try their Chocolate Whiskey!" she recommended.

"Chocolate Whiskey?" Doc echoed in disbelief.

"It's to die for!" she exclaimed.

"Yeah, but am I going to be able to work after eating it?" Doc asked in jest.

"Oh, I'm quite sure you can handle it," she laughed. "I wouldn't call it work, though. We'll just need time with you at the archives, where I can show you what I've recently discovered, and I can answer your questions about the Knights Templar and their lost treasure. But first, enjoy your gelato and let's learn a little about each other."

"I know you're a genius," Doc told her. "What would you like to know about me?"

"I'm no genius, I can assure you" she laughed.

"Well then, you have a lot of awfully smart people fooled," Doc answered.

"I've simply been thorough in my research and have published what I've found," she confirmed. "No more and no less. I take credit only for searching diligently and having the good fortune to find things that have been long lost—or completely forgotten about."

"Well, I can tell you that at least one very smart and successful businessman in the States has invested a great deal of faith and money in the work you're doing at the archives," Doc told her. "As he put it, your work may very well hold the key to solving one of the world's oldest and most legendary mysteries. That's why he sent me."

"But why you?" Madeleine pressed. "Of all the men he could send, he sent you. Why?"

"I'm afraid only he can tell you that," Doc said with a slight shrug. "I've served my country honorably in both military and civilian capacities. I can be trusted with the truth, and I take betrayal personal. I guess that makes me a straight-shooter…and I can understand why my client values that. But you'll have to speak with him for a more complete answer."

"I'd say that pretty well covers it," Madeleine replied. "How do you like the gelato?"

"Delizioso!" Doc acknowledged with a broad smile. "I'm ready to go to work when you are. I need to know everything you can tell me about the Knights Templar and why you're convinced the lost treasure exists. Once I understand that, we can work on where it must be."

Madeleine finished her gelato, wiped her fetching, ruby lips with a napkin, tossed it and her empty gelato cup into the trash, and insisted, "Follow me."

The large stranger Doc had chased on the train from Zurich was watching from the shadows as Madeleine led Doc on a quick, short march across the street to the Vatican. They left him behind as they passed a company of Swiss guards and through the main gate to the security check point, where the Police of Vatican State (The Gendarmeria Corps) thoroughly scrutinized Madeleine's credentials—even though she'd just exited the same gate less than an hour earlier—and closely inspected, and accepted, Doc's bogus passport. Two more Swiss guards carefully scrutinized the pair as they entered the Secret Archives, a magnificent collection of breathtaking, gilded rooms, chambers and corridors filled with seemingly countless books, artifacts, and works of art. As Madeleine led the way to her office, Doc kept stopping to gape in disbelief, and then had to hurry along to catch up with her.

"My eyes are seeing it all, but my mind can't accept that it's all real," Doc remarked breathlessly. "I could never have imagined there was a place of such unbelievable beauty on a scale too grand to believe—all here in one incredible collection."

"It can be overwhelming, can't it?" Madeleine noted. "Okay, I'll give you 'the speech' I give everyone who asks. But you have to promise to follow me without any more interruptions."

"I promise," Doc answered.

"The Vatican's Secret Archives aren't really 'secret.' The word 'secret' comes from a misunderstanding of the Latin word 'secretum,' which actually means 'private.' You see, everything housed here is the 'private' property of the Pope," Madeleine explained.

"You mean it's all the property of the Vatican, right?" Doc still didn't grasp reality.

"No," Madeleine confirmed. "I mean, it's all the Pope's private property. It's the Pope's personal collection of historic and culturally significant documents, books, artwork, and more. Since the 1500s, each successive Pope has literally inherited everything housed here.

"In case you're wondering, the library now includes 53 miles of shelving, 35,000 volumes of catalogues, and 12 centuries worth of documents. The contents of the Vatican's Secret Archives are the stuff of historical legend—but their existence is absolutely real.

"However, it's inescapable that some—perhaps many—documents among the immense volume of material cascading into the library over so many centuries have never been thoroughly authenticated, documented, and organized into manageable order. This barely managed chaos—and occasional discoveries of historic documents—inevitably prompt imaginative folks to concoct sinister theories about what might lie hidden here.

"Now," Madeleine asked, "can we move on to my office and get to the point about the Knights Templar and the treasure you came here to discuss?"

"Absolutely!" Doc confirmed, knowing he sounded like a tourist when he first entered.

Just a few more steps away, Madeleine offered Doc a chair in a surprisingly cramped workspace with her name hanging slightly crooked beside the entrance.

"Have a seat, Doc," she suggested. "We've got quite a bit of material to discuss."

"I'm all ears," Doc assured her.

12

DOYLE'S EQUATION

In Madeleine's remote corner of the Vatican's Secret Archives, she began her story.

"In 1099, Europeans recaptured Jerusalem from Muslim conquerors with the first Crusade. Many Christians with means then made pilgrimages to Jerusalem, which was relatively secure. But the rest of the region wasn't secure, and pilgrims were routinely preyed upon—and many were slaughtered—by bandits lurking between the Mediterranean coast and the Holy Land.

"So in 1119, the Papacy created 'The Order of the Poor Knights of Christ and of the Temple of Solomon—or the Knights Templar, as they came to be known—an impoverished monastic military force to protect Christian pilgrims on the way to and from the Middle East.

"Things got interesting in 1139, when Pope Innocent II pledged all spoils from victories over Muslims to the Knights and exempted the order from tithes, taxes, and local laws. Events became very interesting when the Knights became a favorite charity throughout Christendom and received money, land, businesses, even sons from families eager to help win back the Holy Land.

"The Pope frosted the cake by allowing the Knights Templar to build churches, charge families to bury their dead on church grounds, and annually collect taxes on the graves. Through all these means, and others, for nearly 200 years, the Knights Templar accumulated untold amounts of money and many, many other things of great value," Madeleine explained.

"So a lot of wealth came in," Doc summarized. "But how much went out?"

"As little as possible," Madeleine replied. "Ninety percent of the order's members were non-combatants who either helped manage the order's rapidly growing wealth, or design and build the order's nearly 1,000 outposts and fortifications across Europe and the Holy Land.

"Pope Clement V disbanded the order suddenly, without warning, in the very early morning of Friday, October 13, 1307—the original unlucky Friday the 13th. By that time, the Knights Templar had essentially established the world's first multinational corporation, funded by billions of dollars of tax-free international donations, rents from churches and other properties, and all the spoils gained from every Christian victory over Muslims during the Crusades...yet absolutely none of the vast Knights Templar treasure has ever been found."

"Which is why I'm sitting here this afternoon," Doc chimed in. "You've made a believer out of me, Madeleine. Now, where do I go to find the treasure?"

"Ahhh, that's the $400 billion question," Madeleine teased.

"That's not funny, Madeleine," Doc cautioned, and sat up straight in his seat. "Keeper paid me to fly halfway around the world to help figure out where to find that treasure. You must have narrowed the possible locations down to a very few. I can figure out on my own that it's somewhere safe, somewhere no one's ever looked, or it would have been found long ago. You've studied this for years now. So give me your top three most likely locations, and I'll get going."

"I agree it must be somewhere safe," Madeleine replied, "but I'm not so sure it has to be where no one's ever looked before."

"What's that supposed to mean?" Doc asked incredulously.

"Think about it," Madeleine encouraged. "We're not talking about a pirate's chest. We're talking about something the size of an oil tanker, or a couple hundred box cars. Maybe even the great pyramid of Giza—if it were completely hollow. If you had to hide that much treasure, where would you store it that no one has thought of over all these centuries?"

"I've absolutely no idea," Doc acknowledged, totally exasperated by Madeleine's riddle.

"Me either," Madeleine agreed. "Believe me, researchers and treasure hunters have wrestled with that riddle for centuries. We assume no stone has been left unturned. I wrestled with that truth for the three years I've been here…but last month I questioned it."

"And?!" Doc asked, frustrated and excited at the same time.

"And…I came face-to-face with Sir Arthur Conan Doyle's equation," Madeleine admitted.

"What are you talking about?" Doc was thoroughly lost.

"Doyle famously said—through his famous character, Sherlock Holmes—'Once you eliminate the impossible, whatever remains, no matter how improbable, must be the truth,'" Madeleine reiterated, excitedly.

"Now I'm really lost," Doc surrendered.

"Do you believe the treasure was real?" Madeleine inquired.

"I do," Doc replied.

"Do you believe it's still real?" she questioned.

"I do," Doc insisted again.

"We know the Templars did not keep it in multiple places; they kept it centrally located. We also realize that all the Knights were rounded up and disbanded suddenly and without warning. So they didn't have time to hide it in disparate locations. Yet, after nearly seven centuries of searching, with the aid of many scientific and engineering advancements, treasure hunters and researchers have examined every possible location large enough to contain that much treasure, but no one has ever found it. So no matter how improbable it is, the greatest minds, using state-of-the-art equipment and technology, have somehow missed a mountain of treasure hidden right under their noses…that must be the truth!"

"But there's no way anyone could ever retrace the steps of every treasure hunter and researcher and re-examine every possible clue and hiding place," Doc reasoned.

"That's another truth I wrestled with for the past several months," Madeleine told him. "Then late one night, about a month ago, while tossing and turning in bed half asleep, with my brain exhausted from mulling the facts over and over, I again applied Doyle's equation."

"I'm lost again, Madeleine," Doc confessed.

"Do you agree that hiding that much treasure would require major engineering?" she asked.

"I do," Doc concurred.

"Do you agree that all known Templar engineering has been examined closely?" she inquired.

"I do." Doc thought he might be beginning to sound like a broken record.

"I do too!" Madeleine agreed.

"So I had to admit that I—along with every other researcher and treasure hunter—must be making wrong assumptions about some major feat of Templar engineering," she concluded.

"This isn't helping me," Doc admitted.

"So I reviewed the ruins of major Templar fortresses and churches big enough to be the repository," Madeleine explained. "And I whittled the possible sites down to just three."

"Which ones?" Doc asked hopefully.

"The Templar Base on Arwad Island, off the coast of Tartus, Syria; the Prisoners Tower in Gisors, France; and the Templar Fortress in Acre, Israel," Madeleine clarified.

"All three have tunnels beneath them. And I now believe there could be even more below them than we know."

"Well, re-examining them will take a lot of time and money," Doc answered. "And considerable travel, too."

"Maybe not," Madeleine countered. "I don't believe the Templars inhabited the sites in France and Syria long enough to use either of them as a repository. But the fortress at Acre, Israel, was already in use even before the start of the Crusades. Then the Knights Templar moved their headquarters there when Salah-al-Din's army laid siege to Jerusalem in 1187. Muslim forces didn't catch up to them there until 1291. The Templars held the fortress for over 100 years!"

"That's an awfully long time," Doc articulated Madeleine's point for her.

"It is!" Madeleine agreed. "The Muslims' army laid siege to the city of Acre and the Templars fled to Syria undetected. That too, was a mystery until 1994."

"What happened in 1994?" Doc asked eagerly.

"I was hoping you'd ask," Madeleine advised. "In the spring of 1994, a troop of engineers were on a retreat, of all things, and visited the fortress. They predictably ended up in the bowels of the place and one of them leaned against a wall and inadvertently uncovered a tunnel that had remained hidden for 700 years!"

"Okay," Doc replied flatly. "So they found another tunnel. Big deal."

"It was a very big deal," Madeleine agreed excitedly. "It wasn't an ordinary tunnel: it was the tunnel the Templars used to escape undetected."

"How, exactly?" Doc now needed to know.

"The Templars had carved the tunnel through solid rock, arrow-straight for a quarter mile, all the way to the harbor on Acre's eastern shore."

"A quarter mile?" Doc asked in disbelief.

"Arrow-straight, through solid rock," Madeleine added. "It was an incredible engineering feat for the 13th century. They carved it 20 feet underground, with a smooth stone floor and a vaulted ceiling of hand-hewn stones to prevent cave-ins. To add to the mystery, no one's ever figured out what the Templars did with the immense amount of stone they excavated. This very day, after 700 years of millions of people traipsing through the fortress to take it all in, the number one reason tourists say they visit the fortress is so they can walk through that amazing tunnel all the way to the sea."

"That's amazing alright," Doc suggested. "But I don't see how it has anything to do with the hidden treasure."

"No one else does either," Madeleine agreed. "I didn't either, until I applied Doyle's equation to it."

"Here we go again," Doc sighed in mock frustration.

"The Templars used the fortress as their headquarters for nearly 100 years," Madeleine began the equation. "Follow me closely on this."

"I'm with you so far, Madeleine," Doc replied. "But go slow."

"The Templar devoted an incredible amount of thought, math, science, expense, and plain old-fashioned blood, sweat, and tears to complete the tunnel," Madeleine continued.

"I'm still with you," Doc announced.

"But they never used it as an escape tunnel until they'd occupied the fortress for nearly 100 years. The Templars who conceived and built the tunnel never used it in an escape. The Templars who did use it to escape hadn't conceived it or built it."

"I hope there's a point to this," Doc sighed again.

"Maybe...just maybe, the tunnel wasn't built to get the Templars to the harbor undetected? Perhaps that was just a convenient, happy coincidence on the one day they needed to escape? Maybe...just maybe, they originally built the tunnel to bring things in from all over the Middle East and Western and Eastern Europe, by way of the harbor, undetected for 104 years!"

"OH, MY GOD!" Doc jumped up and shouted. "Oh, my God, Madeleine! You might be on to something very big! But... But... But, where's the treasure?"

"Well," Madeleine answered, "let's assume for the sake of Doyle's equation, that the treasure is there."

"Not Doyle again," Doc complained with a smile.

"Don't knock it," Madeleine shot back. "It's gotten us this far hasn't it?"

"Okay, keep going," Doc encouraged to hurry her along.

"It's there, but still hidden," she suggested. "That has to mean there's a lot more incredible engineering under the fortress that remains to be discovered. And that's where we come in, Doc."

"Whoa!" Doc almost shouted. "That's where I come in. If you're right about the treasure, you've played a huge role in finding it. But your role ends right here in Rome."

"There's no way I'm staying behind," Madeleine argued. "I was a part of this effort before you even knew it existed. Keeper contacted me and brought me on board long before you ever met him. He flew out here to meet with me and close the deal. I made it very clear to him at that time that I intended to accompany whoever he decided to send looking for the hidden treasure. He agreed. And I believe he's a man of his word...just like you. I know you believe it too, or you would never have gotten involved."

"That's all very true, Madeleine," Doc answered. "But I still say there's no way I'm taking you with me...regardless of what Keeper may have agreed to. If you're right about the fortress at Acre, it could be a very dangerous place to be once I get close to the treasure."

"I can take care of myself," Madeleine insisted. "I'm going with you, or I'm going alone. If I've solved the mystery, I deserve to be there when the treasure is finally found. End of story!"

"Well, Madeleine," Doc acknowledged, "I've got to admit. You've got a pretty persuasive story. And the end you put on it is pretty persuasive too. But I have a different story. I accepted this assignment before I knew you existed. Even after I knew you existed, you were just a name and a picture on a piece of paper. My instructions were to connect with you here, in Rome, and work with you to figure out where to go next. I've done everything I've agreed to do concerning you. And now my real work begins. Alone."

"That was quite a speech," Madeleine retorted with sass. "But the truth is you played no part in determining where the treasure might be hidden. That was all me!"

"Here we go with Doyle again!" Doc threw up his hands and headed for the door. "Do what you must. Call Keeper if it makes you feel better. But don't bother telling him to call me, because I won't be answering my phone. I know what I've agreed to do, and by God, I'm going to do it. As far as we know, there could be 400 billion reasons for someone to want to kill me once I get to Acre. I'll have my hands full keeping myself safe. The last thing I need is to have someone else's safety to ensure. And that's the end of my story!"

Doc slammed the door as he left, and Madeleine knocked a stack of paperwork off of her desk in frustration, grabbed her cell phone, and called Keeper.

"Keeper here," Keeper said cheerfully as he rode in the back of his limo on the way to a board meeting. "How are you Ms. Bellarose? Have you and Mr. Hightower made any progress?"

"What in the world did you ever see in that man?!" Madeleine shouted into the phone.

Keeper reflexively pulled his cell phone from his ear and looked at it.

"He's the best there is at what he does, Ms. Bellarose," Keeper calmly replied. "I'm sorry if he's done something to upset you. But I'm convinced he's our surest hope of achieving the goal we share: finding the lost treasure. If you'll just keep that goal in mind, I believe you'll ultimately be glad he's working on our behalf. In fact, I'm sure of it. Goodbye, Ms. Bellarose."

"I hope you're right," Madeleine murmured softly. "Thank you for listening, Keeper."

"Anytime, my dear," Keeper gently replied. "Any time at all."

13

GOD IS NOT PLEASED

D oc marched out of the Vatican at a faster pace than when he entered. He was steaming as he stepped out the front gate onto Via del Pellegrino and desperately looked for a taxi. As he spotted one and waved it down, he suddenly remembered he'd promised to meet Noah for an introduction to HEMA at 3:00 p.m.

It was almost 2:30 when Doc climbed into a taxi and headed for his hotel to quickly change into sweat clothes. When Doc slipped back into the taxi, he took a quick look at Noah's business card and realized he'd no idea how to pronounce the street name. So he simply gave it to the driver, and off they went. Doc stepped onto the curb in front of Noah's training center at 2:57, ready for HEMA… or so he thought.

"Hello, Mr. Hightower!" Noah called out as Doc entered the clean, modern facility.

"Hi, Noah!" Doc replied. "This is quite a place you have here."

"It's practically brand new," Noah said proudly. "And we could already use more room."

"I can see that," Doc agreed. "HEMA is certainly no secret in Rome."

"Well, are you ready to get to work?" Noah asked Doc.

"You bet!" Doc said enthusiastically. "But start slow, okay? I don't want to be embarrassed in front of all these young folks."

"Don't worry, Mr. Hightower," Noah assured him. "We'll take it easy today just to ease you into things until you get the hang of it."

"Sounds good," Doc stated simply.

Doc loved the serious stretching Noah led him through for the first 15 minutes. He'd have been happy to do another 15 minutes, but Noah moved on and introduced Doc to a Swiss longsword with a straight, double-edged, 42-inch blade. It weighed just over three pounds, had a long, two-hand grip with a cruciform hilt, and was perfectly balanced, making it very comfortable to hold and move around with. Noah introduced Doc to the most fundamental moves and reassured Doc that as a new student, he was in control with the pace of the session.

The moves and rhythm quickly awoke Doc's dormant SEAL reflexes and aggressiveness. Doc's innate ability to control and propel his movements and make the sword's balance work for him as he countered Noah's first careful sword thrusts and sweeps.

"Are you sure you haven't done this before?" Noah asked incredulously

Doc laughed, pressed on, and picked up his speed a bit. When he did, Noah reciprocated and the sound of their swords clashing steadily grew louder. Fifteen minutes later, Doc showed no signs of either slowing down or tiring. By then, Noah knew there was something important he didn't know about Doc. So Noah stepped back, raised an arm to signal a pause in the exchange.

"Okay, you've had your fun with me," Noah announced with attitude. "Follow me and I'll embarrass you in private."

He led Doc through a door marked "Exit" and down two flights of stairs to the basement.

"Did I do something to piss you off?" Doc asked with a sheepish grin.

"Best I can tell, it was a lie of omission," Noah admitted cryptically. "My gut tells me you're no stranger to hand-to-hand."

"I've had my share," Doc answered cryptically.

"Oh, you've had more than your share," Noah countered. "Are you sure there's not something more you need to tell me?"

"I haven't got a clue what you're talking about," Doc remarked with a wary smile.

Noah leapt back into action, sweeping and thrusting his longsword faster than ever. He purposely had Doc stuck in a defensive mode and kept him there for five more long minutes, testing his reflexes, balance, hand-eye coordination, and guts. Doc's moves were sometimes a little slow, other times anything but smooth. But all in all, he was clearly not a first-timer to survival by any means necessary.

"You need a lot of practice before you'll be ready for competition," Noah told Doc. "But it's remarkable that you've got me as tired as I have you. Nice work—whoever you are."

"Well, young fella," Doc praised as they took a break and toweled-off, "I guess you've earned the truth."

"People have to earn the truth from you?" Noah asked. "We do have a mountain to climb."

"My real name is John Holiday," Doc began. "I was a U.S. Navy SEAL for three years before being medically discharged a couple of years ago. Two months ago, I was medically discharged from the United States Secret Service. So I've done some push-ups and chin-ups in my life. But I swear, this is the first time I've ever used a longsword."

"But why the phony name?" Noah asked. "What's the point? What are you up to?"

"You might say I'm a freelancer now," Doc confided. "I'm here on assignment for an American client. That's about all I can say at the moment."

"Doc Holiday," Noah said incredulously. "Do you expect me to believe that? You think I never watched TV as a kid?"

"Believe it or not," Doc confessed flatly. "I got 'Holiday' from my folks. And I got 'Doc' when my SEAL team found out I'd graduated from med school before enlisting. It's caused me some grief; but I must admit, it's also a good ice-breaker every now and then."

"I'd be pleased if you called me, Doc, too," Doc encouraged. "This sword's a beauty," he added as he hefted it into the light. "How much does it weigh?"

"A little over three pounds," Noah answered.

"And how much did you say medieval longswords weigh?" Doc asked.

"Twenty to 25 pounds, on average," Noah admitted. "And Templar swords were even heavier—around 30 pounds. But they preferred the broadsword, which was even heavier."

"Why such a heavy weapon?" Doc had to know.

"Templars played for keeps, Doc, just like Navy SEALs."

"How much do you actually know about the Templars, Noah?" Doc inquired sincerely.

"I know those who sent them to do a job only did so if they really wanted it done," Noah said. "During the Crusades, Templars were often advance shock troops: they charged and broke enemy lines, riding heavily armored warhorses. During the Battle of Montgisard in 1177, approximately 500 Templar Knights helped several thousand infantry defeat Salah-al-Din's Muslim army of more than 26,000 soldiers."

"Do you know anything about their lost treasure? Do you think there really is one?" Doc asked as a test.

"Oh, I believe there's one, alright," Noah professed an earnestness that surprised Doc.

"Do you think it will ever be found?" Doc asked.

"No way. Impossible," Noah said emphatically.

"Why do you say that?" Doc pressed.

"Because, like I already said, the Templars played for keeps. So I'm sure when they hid their treasure, they made sure no one would ever find it."

"Have you ever visited a Templar fortress, Noah?" Doc inquired seriously. "Have you ever walked where they walked, and seen their workmanship with your own two eyes, or did you get everything you think you know about them from books?"

Doc was definitely feeling Noah out—pressing to determine if Noah might be of help to him in Acre. Doc had quashed Madeleine's plan to go with him, but he knew his chances for success at finding the treasure were likely to increase with Noah along. Noah could handle himself in a pinch…and this trip just might involve a pinch or two.

"Are you kidding me?" Noah asked excitedly. "I'd jump at the chance to visit one in the Middle East."

"Acre, for instance?" Doc pressed even harder.

"I'd drop everything right here and leave for Acre today," Noah confirmed excitedly. "The Templars headquartered there for a century. I'll bet even their graffiti is amazing!"

"So if you got the opportunity, you'd really take it?" Doc pressed one final time.

"In a heartbeat!" Noah yelled loudly. "I could be packed in an hour."

"Well, I'll make you a deal, big guy," Doc proposed, friend

to friend. "I'm headed to Acre in ten days. I'll take you along if you agree to train me until it's time to go. Deal?"

"Deal!" Noah shouted and high-fived Doc…twice.

"So why are you going to Acre?" Noah asked with genuine interest.

"I've been contracted to perform a careful inspection of parts of the old fortress," Doc conveyed.

"Really?!" Noah could hardly contain himself. "As an architecture student, I'd love that."

"Sounds like we'll be able to do each other some good there," Doc confirmed happily.

"You wanna try a broadsword now?" Noah asked. "I've got a couple that weigh just under 15 pounds. We could give each other quite a workout. What do you say?"

"Bring it!" Doc teased with attitude. He was suddenly pumped about the trip.

Noah brought it alright. He was every bit as pumped about the trip as Doc was. So for another 15 minutes, the pair swung broadswords as though they were broomsticks. Doc was amazed at how heavy the 43-inch weapon could feel after swinging it with all his might for even ten minutes. He was ready for a shower and iced tea.

"I've had it," Doc finally proclaimed when 15 minutes were up.

"You go ahead and shower. I've got a couple of quick phone calls I have to make," Noah cited. "I'll try to catch up with you before you leave."

"Go ahead and take care of business, Noah," Doc told

him. "Supper's on me tonight at the Hotel Medici. Do you know where it's at?"

"Sure do!" Noah alleged.

"Seven o'clock sound good?" Doc asked.

"Perfect!" Noah replied. "See you then."

Forty-five minutes and one shower later, Doc sat on his balcony in his robe and slippers and toweled his wet hair while taking in the view. Being out on the balcony reminded him of his balcony episode in Zurich. It didn't involve any danger—but it could have. And now that he'd collaborated with Madeleine at the Vatican, Doc fully expected the stranger who had stalked him in Zurich to show himself again very soon. In fact, Doc was more than a little surprised the stranger hadn't shown himself already.

If he's any good at his craft, he must know I'll be on the move again soon, Doc deduced in his head. *But I might be giving him too much credit. He might be new at this.*

That chain of thoughts triggered a whole different chain.

The stranger could be a very real danger whether he's a seasoned pro, or a bumbling rookie, Doc knew from experience. *Pros usually don't care who they hurt, and rookies don't know enough to keep from hurting someone accidently.*

Doc was suddenly having second thoughts about involving Noah in the mission.

"He's able to hold his own in controlled settings, like the gym," Doc told himself. "But face-to-face danger is a whole different animal."

After a little more thought, Doc realized he owed it to Noah to lay all his cards on the table and fully explain his purpose for going to Acre, and what he thought could occur during the trip.

"It's the right thing to do," Doc admitted to himself. "I'll tell him everything and let him decide whether to go along or not. My guess is that wild horses couldn't keep him from Acre."

Doc looked at his watch. It was 6:30.

I'll know soon enough, he thought.

He moved down to the bar, just off the lobby, to wait for Noah's arrival.

Noah entered the lobby at exactly 7:00 o'clock. Doc liked that about him. His ambition, positive attitude, and strength were all great qualities, to be sure. But being on time said a lot about what Doc called "outward aware-ness," the ability to consistently organize your personal efforts in ways that respect and support the efforts of others, as well.

"Over here, Noah!" Doc shouted as he stood and waved Noah into the bar.

"What'll you have before we order?" Doc asked.

"A beer's fine," Noah replied.

"Two Heinekens, please," Doc told the bartender.

They talked about sports and HEMA while waiting for a table. Once they got one and ordered, Doc got right to the point.

"What exactly do you believe about the Templar's treasure, Noah?" Doc inquired.

"Well, like I said earlier, I believe it's out there somewhere," Noah answered. "But I've never given much thought to where exactly."

"Why not?" Doc challenged him.

"Because first off, lots of folks smarter than me have looked and never found it."

"What's you're second reason?" Doc pressed for more info.

"The Guardians," Noah said straight up.

"The who?" Doc asked, looking stumped.

"You never heard of the Guardians?" Noah asked in disbelief. "Remember when I told you that Templars were the real deal? When they do something, they do it all the way. Well, the legend is that the Templars still guard their treasure."

"You don't believe that do you?" Doc questioned with his eyes open wide. "I mean, it's a romantic and heroic enough notion. But you can't honestly believe that after 700 years, Templars still guard the treasure…which, by the way, most experts doubt even exists."

"I don't know, Doc," Noah sighed. "I've been perfectly happy not knowing all my life. But now that you're asking, the thought intrigues me. I fear King Philip IV's false accusations of heresy against them may well have stirred God's heart and incited his justice. That evil king was a fool to write an arrest warrant that made the outrageous claim that 'God is not pleased.' It was his desperate attempt to seal the Templars' fate forever. He may have unwittingly done exactly that by invoking the wrath of God. You and I know that to the modern mind, all this seems impossible. But we also know that, 'With God, all things are possible.' So if I ever searched for the treasure, I'd be armed. Still, it would be worth the whole world to stand in the same room with one or two Templar Knights."

"I've been hired to find the lost treasure, Noah," Doc finally disclosed. "I know you're man enough to be a great help to me in the hunt. But are you bold enough?"

"I don't tackle such immense questions over supper, Doc," Noah answered. "We can discuss it during your next lesson in about an hour and a half. But for now, let's eat!"

14

MAGNIFICENT MOUNTAIN

Madeleine had immense questions of her own while she ate dinner alone in her favorite out-of-the-way restaurant that night.

How can this be happening? was the first question she silently asked herself. *Haven't I earned the right to join in the hunt for the treasure that all of my work is finally pointing to? I've invested my life in this search and asked only for the opportunity to see it through!* she shouted in her head. *That's a far greater investment than writing checks in the hope of mere financial gain. Dear God,* Madeleine silently prayed, *please make a way for me in this!*

At that very moment, it seemed like God's answer was approaching her table. She sensed it approaching over her shoulder and turned to see an immense, powerful-looking man come to a stop beside her.

"May I please join you, Ms. Bellarose?" he asked in a deep, resonant voice.

"I…I guess so," was the only safe answer she could muster.

As he pulled a chair close to hers and leaned in close, he placed his huge right hand over hers and met her gaze with a very serious look in his eyes.

"I very much need to speak with you, Ms. Bellarose," he muttered softly but firmly. "Please set your fork down, grab your purse, and come quietly with me now."

Madeleine did as he asked and the dangerous-looking man escorted her across the dining room, out of the restaurant, and into a waiting taxi.

"Who are you?" she asked desperately, as the taxi pulled away from the curb.

"My name's Kenesaw Mountain Matua," he announced. "Most folks just call me Mountain. I'd be pleased if you did too."

The powerful Samoan had abandoned the need for anonymity in this mission. He knew it was moving to a conclusion and he wanted to be recognized for his part when it did.

"But I don't know you!" Madeleine told him defiantly. "And I'm getting really tired of men assuming I'll do as they ask!"

Mountain didn't know about her other interactions with other men that day, and didn't care. He'd reasoned that Doc and the beauty whose supper he'd just interrupted had a plan to find the lost treasure of the Knights Templar, and he planned to force Doc to take him along.

"Where's he going next?" Mountain asked her.

"I don't know what you're talking about," she maintained

through gritted teeth and squirmed as Mountain squeezed her arm with one huge hand.

"I don't have time to play games with you," Mountain assured her. "You don't either, believe me," he added, with a clear double meaning. "Now what's his next move?"

"He thinks he's going to Israel without me," she exclaimed, still gritting. "But he's terribly mistaken."

"You can say that again, pretty one!" Mountain said with a devilish grin. "I just knew that was where the treasure had to be."

"Yeah, sure you did," Madeleine replied sarcastically, despite the painful grip of Mountain's huge hand on her left arm. "Every man in the world is sure he knows all the answers about something or other. That's the way you all are. But somehow, you never quite know what to do about it without getting a woman involved."

"Don't get cocky, sweetheart," Mountain warned ominously. "Your nothing more than my ticket to Israel. I followed him to a gym before fetching you. We're going there now to let him know he's taking the two of us along for the ride."

I'm going after all! Madeleine silently said to God. You actually did it! *You've made a way! Thank you so much!*

Madeleine immediately stopped resisting Mountain's imposition, causing him to think he'd proven that he was the boss.

"I see you understand now," he boasted. "Do as I say and maybe no one will get hurt."

"Don't get too puffed up," she cautioned and moved away

when he freed her arm. "The less you boast now, the less foolish you'll look if it turns out we're wrong about the treasure."

"I've got faith in you, babe," Mountain snickered. "I figure anyone who has what it takes to work at the Vatican must have a lot on the ball. I just hope 'Mr. Hightower' understands that. It'd be a shame if he didn't care enough about you to take us both along with him."

Madeleine hadn't thought of that possibility.

"Even he's not that stupid!" she thought out loud.

"I've known him for a number of years, and I believe you're right," he agreed.

"You know him?!" Madeleine asked, confused. "Then why don't you just ask him to take you along? He'd no doubt put you to good use."

"Don't be too sure," Mountain grunted back at her. "He put me out to pasture once before. This time, I'm calling the shots, and it's for all the marbles. Four hundred billion marbles, that is…give or take a few," he confirmed with a sardonic laugh.

"What do you mean, he put you out to pasture?" she asked.

"We served together as SEALs," Mountain told her, but stared out his window. "I took a bullet for him once, and he couldn't be bothered to write the simple letter it would've taken to return me to active duty."

"I'm very sorry," Madeleine suggested sincerely. "Were the two of you close?"

"I thought we were," Mountain said, still staring out the window.

"But my life went off the cliff when I was mustered out of the SEALs," he contended. "I felt so lost I didn't want to talk to anyone, didn't want anyone to know I was struggling so badly, especially him. So I went off the grid, cut all ties, and just wanted to fade away."

"Have you no family?" Madeleine implored him sadly. "No one to help?"

"None of our team did," he admitted quietly. "We were each other's family…or so I thought. Then Doc let the Navy cut me loose and I fell. I fell real deep…and I feel like I'm still falling."

"I truly wish there was something I could do to help you," Madeleine maintained tearfully.

"You're doing it," Mountain told her and gathered himself. "You're going to get me to Israel. And when we get there, he will know he cut the wrong man loose. He'll regret the day he decided he didn't need me anymore!"

"Are you sure that's what he did?" Madeleine asked him. "He doesn't strike me as that kind of person."

"Yeah, I know," Mountain replied almost angrily. "He fooled me, too…for a while."

"Are you sure he knew you needed him so badly?" Madeleine questioned. "Did you tell him?"

"When the Navy cut me loose, I never looked back," he answered. "I did the only thing I could manage: I put one foot in front of the other and just kept going. I was a week or two shy of livin' on the streets when some guy called me and said he'd cut me a big check if I'd help him find this so-called hidden treasure. I didn't know what the hell he was talkin' about until he showed me some videos about them. Then he told me Doc was working for someone else on the same mission. That was all I needed to know, and here I am. I may not be as smart as him, but I'm here and I've got you. And you're my ticket to that big check...and squarin' things up once and for all!"

"So you're telling me the two of you have gone from brothers in arms to mortal enemies, and he may not even know it?" Madeleine expressed, unable to grasp the concept. "That's insane."

"Watch your mouth!" Mountain grunted. "You don't know me! You don't know what I've been through...or how it feels!"

"You're right," Madeleine admitted. "But I know you're being very hard on yourself walking around with so much anger bottled up inside."

"What do you know about anger?" Mountain grunted again. "You'll see anger when I get in front of him. He doesn't know what anger is yet. But he soon will!"

Madeleine was scared now. She could feel Mountain's anger welling up, and nothing she said helped sooth him.

"I truly do wish there was something I could do to help," she offered one more time.

"I already told you, lady. You're being more help than you can imagine," Mountain laughed almost uncontrollably. "When I walk in with my sidearm to your head, he's going to fill his pants. He'll know who's boss, and we'll be flyin' first class to Israel right along with him."

"Do you really have a gun?" Madeleine asked and began to panic.

"You're damn right, I got a gun!" he spat back at her. "Do you think he's just going to voluntarily cut me in on this huge payday after almost causing me to live on the streets?"

"Don't do this," she pleaded with Mountain. "Let me talk to him, please. I know he'll be reasonable and do the right thing."

"Shut up now!" Mountain told her with a shove. "We're almost there and I got to think!"

While Mountain bowed his head and rubbed his face over and over, Madeleine slipped a hand into her coat pocket and retrieved her cell phone. She was suddenly grateful that she'd been too lazy to set up a PIN for it. She hit the "Keeper" icon and cupped the phone in her hand, hoping Mountain was too distraught to notice it.

"Hello!" Keeper said at his end, but he heard nothing. "Hello?!" he tried again.

He thought Madeleine may have accidently "butt-dialed" him, as his daughter was so fond of calling it. He was about to hang up when he heard Madeleine's voice in the distance.

"Please tell me you're only joking about having a gun on you," she articulated clearly.

Keeper bolted upright out of his oversized executive office chair. His heart rate soared instantly, but he had the presence of mind to resist shouting, "Madeleine, can you hear me?" into the phone. Instead, he just listened intently.

"I don't joke, sweetheart!" Mountain threatened, sounding angrier than ever. "I've got the same gun I used to kill people with when we served together and I saved his ass. And I'll use it on him if I have to. So you better pray that he cares enough about you to do the right thing."

Keeper knew there wasn't time to waste standing at his desk hearing Madeleine's and Doc's lives being threatened. He tapped the Keeper phone icon, set the phone on his desk, and picked up his desk phone.

"Marie, please get President Preston on the phone as quickly as you can," he directed, trying to sound calm.

"I have the President on line one, sir," his executive assistant said anxiously. "I hope everything's alright, sir," she said nervously.

"Everything will be fine, I'm sure, Marie. Thank you," he stated.

"Hello, Mr. President," he announced anxiously.

"Hello, Jonah!" the President remarked in his usual cheerful voice. "What can I do for you?"

"I'm afraid I have an awful mess on my hands, Mr. President," he answered.

"Hang up, Jonah, and I'll call you right back on a secure line," the President commanded.

In a moment, they were talking again.

"I've reason to believe that I have a couple of contractors in mortal danger overseas, Mr. President," he summarized, trying to sound calm. "I need to send them help with as little foreign intrigue or negative exposure for our nation as possible, if you know what I mean."

"Do I know either of them, Jonah?" the President asked.

"I'm afraid you do, Mr. President. John Holiday," he confirmed, knowing it was bad news.

"Where are they?" the President asked abruptly.

"Rome, at the moment," Keeper answered. "But they'll be in Israel by noon tomorrow."

"I've got just the right man in London right now," the President cited. "I can have him on the ground in Rome in two hours. I have Holiday's phone number. Can you give me an address? Is this about the hunt, Jonah?"

"I'm afraid it is, Mr. President," Keeper confirmed.

"Well, look on the bright side," the President suggested cheerfully. "This must mean he's on to something important. If we get this straightened out, it could be very good for all of us! Stay put for the next 24 hours—or until we get this straight—whichever is first, Jonah," the President said. "If I need you on a call, I'll send a car for you immediately. Okay?"

"Okay," Keeper confided nervously. "I can't thank you enough, Mr. President."

"Assuming this goes our way, your efforts on behalf of our nation will be thanks enough, Jonah. Now I must call my guy in London. Stay tuned and God bless, Jonah."

"Goodbye and God bless you too, Mr. President," Keeper acknowledged before the line went dead.

Meanwhile, in that taxi in Rome, Mountain and Madeleine were headed to Noah's gym, and thought no one was the wiser. They couldn't have been more wrong.

"Out!" Mountain barked at Madeleine when the taxi stopped in front of the gym.

She moved as slowly as Mountain would permit, dreading what she knew could be a harrowing experience with Doc and Mountain face-to-face for the first time in over three years. Mountain propelled her forward with two strong, stubby fingers between her shoulder blades. He pushed her through the revolving door and across the marble floor and down two flights of stairs to the basement where Noah was giving Doc a furious introduction to defending against an attacker wielding a seven-foot poleaxe. Mountain locked eyes with Doc as he stepped from the shadowing stairwell with Madeleine cowering in front of him.

"Madeleine?" Doc called to her in disbelief at seeing her at the gym.

"Madeleine!" Noah greeted her, happy to see her at the gym she'd vowed never to visit.

"You know her?" Doc and Noah asked each other incredulously and simultaneously.

"Hello, boys," Madeleine said awkwardly. "I guess you know it wasn't my idea to drop by."

"Everybody shut up!" Mountain yelled, as he pressed the muzzle of his SIG Saur to the back of Madeleine's head. "I'm here to settle a score and to get in line for my piece of the pie!"

"Still got your MK 225, I see," Doc remarked calmly. "Have you been keeping it clean and oiled?"

"Shut up you piece of human waste!" Mountain screamed.

Doc's insides churned when he heard the avalanche of

emotion come rushing out of the man he thought of as a brother, even in that moment.

"Holster the pistol and let's talk, brother," Doc suggested calmly

"The time to talk ended three years ago, Doc!" Mountain shouted and held Madeleine by the hair on the back of her head.

As Doc, Noah, and Madeleine feared, Mountain stood frozen, then dreading Mountain's next move, Q scrambled into the rear seat of an F-22 Raptor at Northolt Royal Air Force Base in West London, and took off for Leonardo da Vinci-Fiumicino Airport, just outside of Rome.

15

THE SECRET WEAPON

Two hours later, as Doc spent listening to Mountain rant about how "the SEALs never call"—even though Mountain had no phone—Doc toweled himself dry from a hot shower and heard the distinct sound of someone opening a can of beer, beyond the bathroom door.

Doc stuck his head out of the bathroom to see who was there and froze, completely speechless, when he saw Q scroll down the cable TV directory, bite into a sandwich, and sip a beer all at the same time.

"I hope you don't mind, Doc," Q said, as though his presence was perfectly normal. "Flying supersonic always makes me hungry."

Doc replied nothing, and continued to stare at Q in disbelief.

"Well, you can at least say hello," Q offered in feigned offense. "After all, our country went to considerable expense to bring me here so I could save your butt."

Stuck on the question of how Q could be in his hotel room, Doc laughed out loud.

"Hello!" he shouted, genuinely amazed. "How? Why?" was all he could say.

"I told you," Q replied. "Your nation sent me to save you —and this mission you've obviously lost control of."

"Everything's going to be just fine—if we don't get killed," Doc admitted with humor.

"What the hell is going on, Doc?" Q asked seriously.

"You know my SEAL history and the backgrounds of my team," Doc began. "It's Mountain. He's had a break-down of some kind. Says I'm responsible for his being 'put out' of the SEALs. He's apparently been bouncing in and out of VA hospitals, rehab centers, and homeless shelters for the past three years, which explains why I couldn't find him. He's armed and extremely dangerous, Q."

"That behemoth is extremely dangerous whether he's armed or not," Q agreed. "But I'm the unknown quantity, so I should be able to get the drop on him and put an end to this."

"It's too risky," Doc warned. "He's got Madeleine in an iron grip, with an MK225 at her head every second."

"Well, I'm not going to just hand him my weapon and see what happens next," Q said flatly. "So we better come up with some kind of plan, quick."

"He took Madeleine to her apartment for the night," Doc explained. "So he let my associate and I go home. We're supposed to meet him and Madeleine at the airport tomorrow morning. He's got a private plane standing by to fly us to Acre in Israel."

"Acre?" Q asked quizzically. "Why Acre?"

"He's apparently on the same hunt for the lost fortune as I am," Doc explained.

"I don't understand," Q admitted.

"It's a long, hard-to-believe story," Doc assured him.

"Well, there's nothing good on TV," Q sighed. "So you've time to explain it to me."

For the next hour and a half, Doc told Q the story and answered his questions.

"Now that that's out of the way, let's hatch a plan over supper," Q said. "You're buyin'!"

Ironically, they went to the same restaurant where Mountain nabbed Madeleine.

"So what do we do, Doc? It's your show," Q acknowledged. "I'm just here to keep you, Madeleine, and that new friend of yours, safe. But I don't know how I'm going to do that if you insist that I stand down."

"I don't want anyone to get hurt, Q," Doc said flatly.

"I don't either friend," Q confessed, "but I may have to reassess my options if this Mountain of yours forces the issue."

"You haven't seen him yet, have you?" Doc asked. "He's a little unsettling when you first meet him. It's hard to believe muscle can be stacked that high and thick. But underneath it all, he's got a heart bigger than he is, Q. He's the closest thing to a brother I've ever had. That's what makes this mess so insane. If he and I were working together, we'd have completed this mission already. We'd either be working on the next mission, or sipping drinks from coconut shells on a beach somewhere. Instead, I have to worry that he—or someone else—will get shot before this is over."

"I don't get paid any more for shooting people, Doc," Q insisted. "You know that. So I'll stand down as long as I possibly can. But the President is anxiously waiting to hear I've accomplished my mission...namely, keeping you and Ms. Bellarose safe and sound."

"I know, Q," Doc said again. "I know."

"Well, I know I'm tired," Q announced. "I was thrilled to see you got a room with two double beds. By the way, I snore."

"Oh, that's just great!" Doc said and rolled his eyes.

"What time is Reveille?" Q asked.

"0500," Doc clarified.

"What?!" Q shot back. "What's the rush? I thought you said he has a private plane!"

"He's a SEAL, Q," Doc confirmed simply. "Welcome to the team."

"What's your ETA in Acre?" Q warily asked.

"0800 Acre time," Doc answered. "While you're in the shower, I'll figure out how we get you on the plane."

"Don't bother," Q answered. "I'll call Washington and have them arrange to fly me to Acre. I'll be there waiting for you."

Q showered, shaved, arranged a flight, got three hours of sleep, and was gone by 0300. Doc joined Mountain, Madeleine, and Noah at the airport a little after 0600 and boarded a chartered jet to Acre. He wanted to tell Madeleine and Noah about Q, but Doc dared not risk Mountain overhearing him. So for now, Q was Doc's secret weapon.

"I believe we can still work this out to everyone's benefit, Mountain," Doc suggested calmly. "If we don't reach some understanding now, and we find out there really is no treasure in Acre, I don't know how we'll ever undo all of this and pretend it never happened."

"That's not my plan," Mountain said softly, locking eyes with Doc.

"Then what is your plan, brother?" Doc asked.

"DON'T YOU EVER CALL ME BROTHER AGAIN!" Mountain shouted and jumped to a standing position just inches from Doc. "You weren't there when I needed you the most, Doc! Why?"

"You do know that I got shot too, right?" Doc thought Mountain must have known.

"No!" Mountain retorted with a sympathetic tone. "When? Where?"

"Aboard the USS *Ronald Reagan*," Doc revealed. "The mission you couldn't join us for. I thought you knew. I ended up in Walter Reed for several weeks. Then I got mustered out just like you did."

"Damn bastards!" Mountain shouted to no one in particular.

"Two years later, I caught another bullet working with the Secret Service," Doc added. "So it was more time in the hospital and rehab. And the whole time, I wrote to you again and again. I tried to reach you by phone too, but no one knew where you were."

"I'm sorry, Doc!" Mountain declared sincerely. "I figured you forgot about me...that you were too busy looking out for yourself to make sure I got a fair shake. You always did that for me in the SEALs, Doc. But after I left, I never heard from you. I thought it was your fault...but it was mine."

"Easy Mountain," Doc clarified, as he tried to wrap an arm around Mountain's massive shoulders. "We're together now, and brothers again. I love you, Mountain."

"I love you too, Doc!" Mountain replied and momentarily squeezed the air out of Doc's lungs.

"Partners?" he asked Doc and stuck his hand out for a shake.

"Partners!" Doc replied and shook Mountain's hand enthusiastically. "So tell me, Mountain, who helped you find me?"

"A group of businessmen from Somalia," Mountain admitted.

"Somalia? What kind of business are they in?" Doc asked.

"Shipping," Mountain said, simply.

"What kind of shipping?" Doc pressed him.

"I don't know," Mountain mumbled with a shrug. "They just said shipping."

"What did they ask you to do?" Doc asked urgently.

"They asked me to help them find the treasure you are looking for," Mountain said.

"What did they promise you?" Doc needed to know.

"They promised to help me find you," Mountain confirmed with a smile.

"And they paid your expenses?" Doc began putting the pieces together.

"They're rich, Doc," Mountain verified. "And they want to get richer."

"So they paid for everything?" Doc pressed the point.

"Everything," Mountain acknowledged. "Did I do something wrong, Doc?"

"Did anyone travel with you?" Doc pressed some more.

"Sometimes," Mountain said. "Sometimes not."

"How about this time?" Doc continued pressing.

"Nobody came with me this time, Doc," Mountain specified.

"How do you contact them when you need something?" Doc asked.

"They gave me this cell phone," Mountain handed it to him.

"Do they ever call you?" Doc pressed some more.

"Once in a while—but not very often," Mountain told him.

"Do you ever call anyone else?" Doc probed again.

"Who would I call, Doc? I don't even have your number," Mountain specified.

"Do they know you found me?" Doc asked.

"I didn't tell them. So I don't think so, Doc," Mountain replied.

"But they paid for the plane that bought us here, right?" Doc asked, urgently.

Mountain just nodded. "Yes."

"Can I hang onto your phone for a little while?" Doc asked him.

"Sure!" Mountain alleged.

As Doc tucked the phone into a pocket, just one word was on his lips: "Pirates!"

"We'll be on the ground in 20 minutes," the pilot announced over the intercom.

"So now we are one army," Doc excitedly announced to the group. "Our chances of success just increased about 100-fold."

"I can't imagine what you could do with a broadsword, Mountain," Noah exclaimed.

"What's a broadsword?" Mountain asked.

"Show him, Noah," said Doc with a laugh.

Noah opened the case he'd brought containing two broadswords and handed one to Mountain. "You hold it with two hands," Noah told him.

"Why?" Mountain asked innocently, as he raised the huge,

heavy sword over his head like an ordinary garden rake, with just one hand.

"Forget it," Noah said and shook his head at Doc.

"So can I relax and stop worrying about getting shot now?" Madeleine asked.

"I'm very sorry if I scared you, Miss," Mountain told Madeleine sincerely. "I was just mad, that's all."

"Well, please don't get mad around me again," Madeleine urged him just as sincerely.

The team deplaned and piled into a waiting SUV that took them directly to The Citadel of Acre, an ancient fortress the Ottoman forces built upon the foundation of the Templar fortress they had sacked—and the Templars had hastily abandoned—in 1291.

Doc suddenly felt very strange. He'd never been so unprepared for a mission in his life. For all he knew, his team was headed toward what might be the largest treasure trove that ever existed, and they'd absolutely no plan for what to do once they got there.

"Mountain, I'm going to have to count on you like never before," Doc told his brother-in-arms, as genuinely as he'd ever said it.

"You can count on me, Doc," Mountain confirmed with a warm grin. "Like always!"

"Noah, I need you to stick close to me," Doc instructed. "I'm assuming this will take at least two trips. But this trip, we're just simple tourists. So the weapons stay here."

"Got it, Doc!" Noah replied.

"Madeleine, you must be your most attractive self ever," Doc told her.

"Now you tell me," she sighed. "I would've taken more time this morning…curled my hair, brought my makeup."

"You look gorgeous!" Noah told her with real meaning.

Doc sensed something more was going on between those two, and it made him happy.

"Just don't forget I'm far, far more than a pretty face!" she told Noah, emphatically.

"Far, far more!" Noah echoed and grinned.

"Far, far more!" Mountain repeated, in turn.

"Far, far more!" Doc echoed too, and the three of them laughed hysterically.

"Far, far more indeed!" Madeleine reiterated, convinced that she'd made her point.

The more Doc thought about it, the more comfortable he now was with the situation they faced. It seemed perfectly natural to scout the fortress while pretending to be tourists. He knew they'd blend right in…except for Mountain, of course. Like Madeleine, he'd be a distraction, which would enable the team to wander and roam off the beaten path as much as they wanted. Everything seemed to fall into place. Even a possible visit from pirates didn't surprise him.

"Nothing just happens," Doc whispered to himself with a smile. "Everything happens for a reason."

16

WHO GOES THERE?

Doc gave Madeleine the money for their tickets, and she began flirting immediately, starting with the college-age ticket-seller. Then she fluttered her eyelashes at the tour guide.

"The poor old guy doesn't stand a chance," Doc chuckled, confident that he, Noah, and Mountain would be able to wander far and wide in the corridors and in the tunnels below. Their disadvantage was not having any idea what they were seeking.

"What are we looking for?" Mountain asked him, while Noah listened intently.

"Anything that looks unusual among the bricks and mortar," Doc said, winging it.

"According to Madeleine, if we find any hint of a hidden chamber, we'll probably locate it beneath the fortress, in the lowest levels of the tunnels. Remember, the chamber we're looking for could be the size of two or three football fields, with walls perhaps fifty feet or more high. Those dimensions alone could mean the opening is large, maybe big enough to drive a bus through, or even a train? So if we look for an opening that large, we've got a better chance of finding it than all the searchers who were never sure of where to check...or what to search for."

Doc looked up from the team and noticed Q buying a ticket. Moments later, he wandered in their direction and ended up in their midst.

"Folks," Doc whispered, "I want you to meet a very good friend of mine, U.S. Marshal Quinton Marshall."

"Marshal Marshall?" Noah asked out loud.

"Just call me Q," Q insisted.

"So now we're one, tight-knit group," Doc said, optimistically, "and we're about to go to our Plan B."

"I didn't know we had a Plan B," Q said with surprise.

"I'm creating it right now," Doc explained with a nervous grin and pulled a bag of pistols from under his seat.

"Regrettably, we're all going to carry a pistol."

"I'm fine with a broadsword," Noah insisted.

"Fine," Doc agreed, "but it won't fit under your shirt, so leave it in the vehicle for now."

Everyone else, except Madeleine, took a pistol.

"I don't feel comfortable carrying one," she explained to Doc.

Moments later, the dozens of tourists began following the guide with a microphone into the fortress. It oozed history and legend, distracting everyone in the crowd, just as Doc had hoped. The team moved so freely around the edges of the crowd that Doc had to work hard to resist the temptation to break away completely and venture into roped-off areas that seemed to be around every corner.

This is beginning to feel like a game of find the needle in the haystack, he thought to himself. *Stay positive and keep looking*, he reminded himself.

Over the next forty-five minutes, Doc had to give the other members of his team the same pep talk, along with a couple of reminders. The challenge was daunting. The light was terrible. The wall surfaces were uneven and crumbling, making it nearly impossible to detect telltale seams where they perhaps shouldn't be.

"This could take months of looking," Noah signed, sounding ready to surrender.

"Especially when we're not at all sure there's anything to find," Q added.

"Here's something!" Madeleine rasped as low as she could.

Doc examined what appeared to be an odd overlapping of stones with no apparent function or purpose at the very corner of a wall just past a rope meant to keep tourists at a distance. He used the flashlight on his phone to look for a similar overlap further along the 20-foot wall. He almost shouted to the others when he found the exact same overlap pattern in the rough-cut stones. He waved his light to get their attention.

"I think we've found a door," he told them excitedly.

"Yeah, but how does it open?" Q asked no one in particular.

"Just try to push, tap, pull, or slide every stone in that area of the wall," Doc advised, barely containing his excitement.

First five minutes went by, then ten, then twenty, and the team made no progress looking for a trigger mechanism of some kind. By then, Doc was sure the tour had moved far enough along the route without them. It gave some comfort to know they didn't seem to be missed. Another ten minutes passed, and they still hadn't found a way to open the wall. Doc was beginning to fear they'd be discovered if they lingered much longer.

"Hey! Hey!" Mountain whispered loudly.

As seems typical in monumental discoveries, a happy accident happened. Mountain leaned against the opposite wall, traced a finger along a mortar line, and apparently drew a critical pattern totally by accident. As he completed the pattern, the stones within the pattern recessed about a half-inch into the wall. But nothing else happened.

"Now what?" Noah asked as the team stared at the recessed stones.

"How about this?" Doc asked, as he pushed on the stones a little harder.

"Holy shit!" Q yelled as the wall across from the trigger slid left to reveal an opening just wide enough to squeeze through.

"Let me by," Doc said excitedly as he hurriedly pushed his way to the opening and stuck his phone's flashlight into the opening.

"It's cavernous!" Madeleine revealed excitedly.

"I'm going in!" Doc announced, unable to help himself.

Inside the opening, Doc was sure he saw a faint light coming from the farthest reaches of a cave that seemed to be about the size of a commercial aircraft hangar. Doc turned out his light to get a better feel for the darkness.

"There's faint light coming from the far end of this. I'm sure of it," he shouted to the others. "Come on in, the water's fine!"

One by one, they squeezed through the opening. Doc turned his light back on and it was obvious the large door was engineered to open much wider.

"It must be stuck," he thought out loud. "Let's try to close it behind us in case someone comes looking for us."

"But what if we can't reopen it?" Madeleine asked.

"In for a penny, in for a pound," Doc shrugged and signaled Mountain to close the door.

"Wait a minute," Q said urgently. "Noah's not here."

"Maybe he got cold feet," Mountain suggested.

"I doubt it," Doc remarked. "I'll bet he went back to the vehicle for something."

Doc didn't say it out loud, but he figured that Noah went back for his broadsword. It just made sense that the HEMA fanatic would want to have it handy…just in case.

"Who goes there?!" Doc thought he heard someone say far off in the darkness.

"Did you hear that?" he asked the group.

"Hear what?" Mountain asked. "I didn't hear a thing."

"Me either," Madeleine said.

"I can only hear my heart pounding," Q admitted.

"Who goes there?!" Doc heard again, slightly louder.

He signaled for silence and they crouched in the darkness, waiting to hear…someone.

"Who goes there?!" they finally all heard.

Almost comically, they grabbed onto one another in panic.

"Who goes there?!!" the voice asked again, more urgently.

"Who wants to know?" Mountain yelled back.

"Who goes there?!" was the only reply.

"Somebody thinks he's funny, but I'm going to shut him up if he doesn't stop," Mountain cautioned to no one in particular.

"Who goes there?!" came from the dark yet again.

Wiser now, the team ignored the voice and inched their way toward it in the dim light. To save battery power, Doc only turned his phone's light on occasionally and briefly to ensure they weren't about to misstep in the darkness. The others soon did the same, and they began to take turns turning their lights on along the way. Then suddenly, they thought they heard footsteps approaching from behind.

"Hey, guys! It's me!" Noah called out to the team. "I think we're in the clear. It looks like the place is closed for the night."

"Won't they see our vehicle and come looking for us?" Madeleine asked.

"Maybe," Doc said, "but they won't find us in here."

"I don't know if that's a blessing or a curse," Q mumbled.

"Who goes there?!" the voice rang out more clearly now.

The team was moving closer to whoever it was that appeared aware of their presence.

"Humble pilgrims, Good Knight!" Noah called out loudly.

Doc looked over his shoulder at Noah, as if to ask *Are you stupid, or what?*

"Be ye Christian?" Keeper was now at least asking a different question.

"Christians!" Q called out. "That's right, isn't it guys?" he asked innocently.

"How many are ye?" Keeper asked.

"Five!" Madeleine called out.

"You've brought a maiden with you! Has the journey been kind?" the voice asked.

"Very!" Doc finally joined the strange conversation.

"You're armed," the voice said.

"He's spotted my sword," Noah whispered.

"You had to bring a sword, for cryin' out loud?!" Doc protested.

"We talked about this," Noah shot back. "You may be glad I did before this is over."

"You can see us, but we can't see you," Madeleine said to the voice. "Show yourself."

"I shall, if and when I so wish," the voice answered, suddenly sounding as though it was in their midst.

The whole team jumped and gasped, shocked and surprised in the darkness.

"For what purpose have you come?" the voice was now clearly among them.

"Is anybody getting this on their phone video?" Q asked.

"For what purpose have you come?" the voice calmly inquired again.

"We've heard of your storehouse," Doc articulated, cryptically.

"Are you in need of help?" the voice asked.

"We wish only to see it," Doc lied.

"If that was our wish, we wouldn't keep it down here," the voice advised.

"He's got a point," Mountain chimed in, and said, "We don't believe it's real."

"That's a pity," the voice replied.

"We wish to assure the world the Knights Templar are exactly who they claim to be," Doc said.

"The world knows who we are," the voice replied.

"That's another good point," Mountain noted.

"We won't leave until we see it," Noah stated confidently… but scared.

"Who dares test me?" the voice called out. "Show yourself, pilgrim."

Noah slowly walked to the front of the team, the grip of

his broadsword showing over his right shoulder, secured in its back strap sheath.

"Draw your sword," the voice commanded.

"Don't do it, Noah, please!" Madeleine pleaded and grabbed his arm.

"Draw your sword, if you wish to ever see that which is hidden here," the voice directed.

Noah reached over his shoulder, grasped its grip, and slowly drew it from its sheath.

"Careful, Noah," Doc whispered. "Move slowly. This may just be a test of your nerve."

"I've got this," Noah said with a firm, steady voice.

"You're close to that which you seek," the voice confirmed.

"Show it to me," Noah declared in a firm, loud voice.

"Earn it!" the voice demanded.

"Must I slay you?" Noah asked in a threatening tone.

"You cannot kill me," the voice assured him. "But I can kill you."

"Stop this, Noah!" Madeleine pleaded. "This isn't a game!"

"But what if you don't succeed?" Noah asked the voice.

"You may have your wish," the voice uttered.

"Show yourself!" Noah demanded.

But no one appeared.

"Are you a coward?" Noah shouted. "Show yourself."

Faintly at first…and then brilliantly, the knight appeared. Resplendent in shiny Templar armor and a bright, white linen tunic emblazoned with a blood-red cross, the knight was at least seven feet tall, and looking to be the fittest, fiercest Knight Templar to ever walk the earth.

"Dear God in heaven, have mercy on our souls," Madeleine knelt and whispered soft and low as she made the sign of the cross and pulled her tiny gold cross out from under the bodice of her dress. Seeing the cross, the knight knelt also and took off his helmet.

"You may have my gold cross if you so wish," Madeleine told the knight.

"We have more gold than silver, more silver than anyone else in the world," the knight confirmed.

"But what will become of it?" Madeleine asked him. "Does it honor God, or does it just lie here and demand that you stay with it…stay and be its slave, instead of its master? And where are the others, while you guard this way with your very life?"

The knight stared at the stone floor he was kneeling on and said nothing.

"Has no one ever asked you these questions?" Madeleine boldly asked.

"I've asked them myself," the knight said softly, still staring at the cold, stone floor.

"So where are the others?" she inquired again. "Do you even know?"

"They promised they'd return," the knight reiterated sadly.

"How long have they been gone?" Madeleine asked compassionately.

"A very long, long time." The knight sounded weary now.

Madeleine rose to her feet and approached him. When she was at his side, she reached out to put her hand on his shoulder, but it was like a vapor. Startled, she looked at Noah over her shoulder with a glance that beckoned him to join her. Noah stood beside her and saw the knight's mist for himself. He placed the palm of his hand where it should have rested atop the knight's head, but that too was like vapor.

Then Doc joined them, reached out his hand, and saw for himself that the knight was more like smoke than flesh and blood.

"This isn't a man," Doc softly whispered to them. "This is something else entirely."

17

THE SOUND OF TROUBLE

"What's your name?" Madeleine asked the knight.

"Julienne Artimus LaDevereux," he told her. "I'm French. But I fear I may never see France again. What's your name, m'lady?"

"Madeleine Bellarose," she confirmed.

"Are you also French?" he asked with interest.

"I am!" she admitted. "And I was in France this past spring."

"Is it still beautiful?" he questioned her.

"Very," she answered quickly. "When was the last time you were there?"

"The winter of 1309," he revealed solemnly.

Madeleine shared her startled expression with Noah and Doc. The three of them knew this encounter was impossible. Yet, here he was.

"When will your work be done here?" Madeleine asked him.

"When the others return," he answered flatly.

"Does it not concern you that they've been gone so long without sending you word?" she probed him.

"My orders are to guard the treasure until they return," the knight announced resolutely.

"They've returned," Madeleine told him, softly.

The weary knight slowly shifted his gaze from the floor to Madeleine.

"But I don't see them," he told her.

"We'll bring them to you," she promised, and led the team away.

"What are you doing?" Doc asked in frustration.

"I'm trying to free him," she confessed.

"But how?" Doc still struggled.

"I think I know a way," Noah acknowledged. "Follow me."

As he led them back toward the chamber's entrance, Noah explained his hunch.

"We know the Templars built a secret tunnel more than a quarter-mile long, through solid rock, all the way to the harbor. It took years," he noted. "In the meantime, they needed a keep."

"What's a 'keep'?" Q asked.

"Basically, it's a panic room," Noah said.

"What the heck is a panic room?" Mountain inquired.

"A safe room," Noah specified. "A place the Templars could retreat to, a place where they could 'keep' things they would need if the fortress was ever surrounded or overrun by the enemy. They stocked it with clean food, water, weapons, armor…and uniforms."

As Noah finished explaining, he stopped beside a boulder that hid what he guessed was the opening to a safe room… his personal idea of a "hidden treasure."

"If my hunch is right," Noah explained, "the Templar will soon be relieved of his duty."

Doc approached the boulder, considered its size and weight, then stepped aside and said, "Mountain…do your thing."

Skeptically, Noah, Madeleine, and Q watched Mountain stride to the boulder. They quietly doubted while he found edges he could grip tightly in his hands, planted both feet, put his entire body into it, and heaved and pushed and grunted until the boulder began to roll. The others quickly joined in and helped push the boulder completely aside.

Noah excitedly stuck his head in the opening while Doc shined his phone light inside.

"BINGO!" Noah shouted.

The team followed closely behind Noah into a large room filled with aisle after aisle of carved wooden shelves that reached from floor to ceiling. It held everything from cooking oil to lamp oil, from water to grain, from chamber pots to blankets, but the team found no uniforms, no armor, and no weapons.

"They must be somewhere else," Q reasoned.

"But there should at least be some in the keep," Noah argued.

Refusing to abandon the search, Noah returned to the back wall. He leaned in close and ran the palms of his hands over the stone. There wasn't even a tiny seam, not a crack.

"We must be missing something," he insisted.

"Give it up, Noah," Doc said. "It's a dead end."

"There's something strange about these shelves on the back wall, Doc," Noah surmised. "All the other shelves in the room have no dividers. People in one aisle can pass things through to people in the next aisle."

"So?" Doc asked with a shrug.

"Sooooo," Noah thought out loud, "why do these shelves on the back wall have one?"

"Who knows!" Doc said dismissively.

"Let's find out," Noah encouraged, and began yanking on the shelving. "Give me a hand, Mountain," he pleaded.

Mountain stepped alongside Noah and the two of them were able to pull the shelving slightly away from the back wall.

"I knew it!" Noah shouted. "It's a door!"

The rest of the team excitedly helped swing the shelving aside to expose a doorway to a room filled with racks of brightly shining Templar armor, various weapons, and shelves filled with white linen Templar tunics.

"You did it, Noah!" Madeleine shouted as she leapt into his arms and kissed him.

"I'm sure glad I kept looking!" Noah announced breathlessly and returned Madeleine's kiss.

"I had a feeling there was something going on between you two," Doc chuckled.

"Time to dress up!" Q said excitedly.

The team hurriedly helped one another with the cumbersome process of donning the awkward, heavy armor, and then graced it with the classic Knights Templar tunic.

"No way am I missing this picture!" Madeleine proclaimed as she fished her phone out from under her armor, propped it on a shelf, and set the timer. Then she ran to the team and stood with an arm around Noah's waist, while he pulled her close and everyone smiled.

CLICK!

"That's it, folks!" Doc said. "We didn't come for pictures."

"We didn't come to be knights either," Q noted with a touch of pride. "But look at us."

"I wish SEAL Team Warrior could see us now!" Mountain shouted to Doc.

"We'll have to send them a copy of the photo!" Doc laughed. "Here we go!" he said and led the team out of the room, past the boulder, and back in the direction of the Templar guard.

"Do you really think this will work?" Doc asked Noah.

"I've no idea," Noah admitted. "But what have we got to lose?"

"Our lives!" Q answered.

"Get a grip, folks," Doc encouraged. "He's not a living, breathing human being."

"But he hears us and sees us, Doc," Q maintained. "He talks to us, answers questions, and worst of all, he disappears and reappears."

"I agree," Doc said. "But whatever he is, and no matter how tough he talks, he hasn't posed a danger to us yet. So as far as we know he's just saying what he's been told to say, like a glorified scarecrow."

"Never seen a scarecrow so fancy," Mountain specified.

"But he's been there for 700 years," Madeleine reiterated. "So he must be there for a reason. Like you always say, Doc, everything happens for a reason. And I personally believe the reason is the treasure."

"Well, like Q said just a minute ago, the knight hears us and sees us," Doc replied. "Hopefully, he's so feeble—and his eyes are so bad—he'll believe we're Knights Templar arriving to relieve him."

"If this works, you just gotta know he's harmless," Mountain suggested.

"And if he's harmless, the treasure will soon be ours," Doc expressed.

"Well, whatever he is, we're about to find out," Noah said as they returned to the spot where they first encountered him.

"Who goes there?" the familiar voice boomed.

"Here we go again," Mountain sighed.

"Who goes there?" the voice asked again.

"We've returned, brother!" Madeleine called out to the voice.

"Is it true?!" the voice called out and cracked ever so slightly.

"It is!" Madeleine shouted happily. "You've done your part, brother. And we've come to do ours! You're officially relieved!"

"That didn't sound very official to me," Q whispered to Noah.

"No?" Noah replied sarcastically. "Well, you hang out here for the next 700 years and see how official it has to sound when your relief arrives."

"He's got a point," Mountain chimed in.

"Would you please knock it off?" Q protested to Noah.

"I'm just trying to help," Mountain explained.

"Put a sock in it, guys!" Doc told the three of them. "It's show time."

The team stood at attention, chests out, shoulders back, while the old knight walked among them.

"Steady team," Doc whispered to help calm them. "We get through this, we're home free."

The old knight walked slowly and appeared to look each of them over closely. He looked at Mountain the longest, eye-to-eye for quite a while.

What's he looking at? Doc wondered silently. *Does he suspect we're the bunch that were just here trying to get past him, or is he trying to remember us as comrades he once knew, 700 years ago? What's taking him so long to decide what he'll do?*

"You've been a long time, and I'm glad you've returned," the old knight finally confessed. "By your leave, I now surrender the watch to you to do as you will," he said, and pounded a fist to his heart in salute. "May God be with you, comrades."

"And also with you!" Madeleine replied, forcefully.

The group was transfixed, as the old knight walked away, in the direction of the Templar Tunnel. His glow didn't dim as he walked farther and farther away, into the darker and darker recesses of the huge cavern. He became smaller and smaller as he walked, which left the group wondering if he wasn't only getting farther away, but also steadily shrinking and would soon be gone forever. And in minutes, he was.

"My grandkids are never going to believe this story," Q said.

"Nobody will," Doc declared. "That's why we're never going to breathe a word of this. Got it?! If any of you ever tell someone in authority about this, I can guarantee you'll spend the rest of your life in a padded room. So forget it. Focus on finding the treasure. Now let's get moving."

"Shouldn't we change first?" Madeleine asked, hopefully.

"Focus!" Doc directed even louder. "How long could it possibly take to determine whether or not a pile the size of a hundred or so boxcars is here? Pick a direction and get moving, people!"

The five of them fanned out and the search began. Doc was right. It didn't take long.

"Hey, guys!" Mountain's voice echoed. "Come here and look at this!"

Mountain found an earthen pyramid about a quarter-mile away.

"I don't know, guys," Q said warily. "It kinda looks like a landfill to me."

"I think not," Madeleine professed. "There's nothing but solid rock all around us. The dark soil you see was hauled in here. Who goes to that much trouble?"

"Oh, screw this!" Doc said with exasperation. "Hand me your broadsword for a minute, please, Noah," he asked.

"Be gentle with it," Noah kidded as he handed the sword to Doc, handle first.

Doc pivoted toward the mound and anxiously shoveled the soil, throwing huge clumps over his shoulders. Approximately two feet down, the sword struck harder material and made distinct clanking, jangling noises. Excited, he reached into the hole and withdrew a burlap bag he estimated to weigh about twenty pounds.

"I'll give you the honors of showing us what's in the bag," he told Madeleine.

Caught off guard by the weight of the bag, Madeleine clutched it to her stomach with one arm and reached inside with her free hand. As she did, she froze and her face grew flushed as she sucked air into her lungs and held it.

"Well?" Noah prodded her.

"Come on, Madeleine!" Q shouted when she failed to respond to Noah's prodding.

"It's gold alright!" Doc said, as he took the bag from Madeleine, reached in, threw a fistful of gold into the air, and shouted, "I guess you could say I let the cat out of the bag!"

Noah knelt at the hole Doc had dug and shoveled dirt with his gauntlet-gloved hand to satisfy himself that the bag Doc pulled out of the hole wasn't a fluke. In a moment, he lifted a bag of similar size and weight from the hole. Next, Madeleine was caught up in the excitement and plunged a hand into the hole. She pulled a much smaller bag out and emptied dozens of large, uncut diamonds into Noah's cupped hands.

"Dear God in heaven!" Madeleine gasped and laughed and gulped some more.

She and Noah clutched their bags as they gazed again at the immense size of the mountain standing before them.

"Mountain, can you please come here a minute?" Doc asked quietly.

"Sure, Doc. What's up?" Mountain asked.

"Could you please do that stride thing you do to measure distance for me?" Doc whispered.

"You bet!" Mountain confirmed and began taking long strides along the base of the pyramid.

"We have to talk," Q whispered to Doc.

"Well, talk," Doc said.

Q led Doc a few yards away from the others and showed him one of the hundred or so gold coins he'd just thrown into the air as though they were yesterday's popcorn.

"Do you know what this is?" he asked Doc, cryptically.

"Yeah, it's a gold coin," Doc shrugged. "It's probably worth good money, right?"

"What would you consider 'good money,' Doc?" Q quietly inquired.

"I don't know," Doc said. "Maybe a couple hundred dollars?"

"That coin you're holding is a Byzantine Gold Solidus Justinian II, stamped somewhere between 685 and 695 A.D. That's Jesus on the front, there," Q confirmed.

"Jesus!" Doc remarked, a little too loudly for Q's liking.

"Doc, trust me on this, you're going to have to keep your voice down…and your heart rate, too," Q whispered to him.

"What are you talkin' about, Q?" Doc asked in exasperation. "Just get to the point, okay?"

"Doc, how many of these coins would you guess are in a bag this size?" Q questioned quietly.

"I don't know, Q," Doc sighed. "A couple thousand maybe?"

"My guess, judging by the weight, it's closer to 5,000," Q corrected him.

"Now, guess how much that one coin you're holding in your hand is worth," Q requested.

"I'll guess $300," Doc sighed. "So am I right?"

"Not nearly," Q announced with a huge grin. "One of these coins is easily worth $5,000."

"FIVE THOUSAND DOLLARS!" Doc shouted. "Are you kidding?!" Doc yelled again.

"So how much does 5,000 multiplied by 5,000 equal, Doc?" Q toyed with him.

"Stop this right now, Q!" Doc said, visibly upset. "Just tell me how much!"

"This one bag is probably holding $25 million dollars in gold coins," Q whispered low.

Mountain jogged over to Doc and Q after pacing around the base of the pyramid.

"So how big is it?" Doc asked him.

"Roughly 150 feet square," Mountain alleged.

"Thanks, Mountain!" Q praised. "Doc and I will join you with the rest of the team shortly.

"So don't think about this too much," Q said. "But take a minute right now and look at the size of that pyramid. If it's 150 on a side at its base, I'd have to guess that it's at least six, seven stories high, wouldn't you agree?"

"Oh, um, ummm, at least!" Doc began to stutter.

"Now let it go and focus on getting us all out of here and safely back home, Doc," Q suggested.

"Cause if you give too much thought to what we've found here, you'll either go into cardiac arrest... or prison. I suggest that we take a few of these coins back to D.C. as samples, put the rest back where we found them, and cover up the hole so no one will know we were ever here."

"I don't know, Q," Doc began to waver. "I don't think it's wise to walk away from this site. What if someone else stumbles onto it, now that we've gotten rid of the guardian? Or worse, what if someone else is looking for it? I think Mountain might have a heap of trouble descending on him shortly…and on us along with him."

"What are you talking about?" Q asked.

"I'm pretty sure he somehow crossed paths with Somali pirates," Doc conveyed. "I mean, I think they deliberately crossed paths with him to get to me. Mountain didn't find me on his own, Q. God love 'em, he's just not up to it. But whoever he was working for fed him sensitive info about my whereabouts and hints at what I was probably up to. That took organization, contacts, and money. He told me they're Somali businessmen engaged in the shipping business. What's that sound like to you?"

"The sound of trouble," Q agreed.

Doc dropped a dozen of the gold coins into one of his gauntlet gloves, and then returned the bag to its place in the pyramid. Q convinced Madeleine and Noah to do the same. Then he and Doc refilled the hole and smoothed the earth to conceal the fact that it had ever been disturbed. Reluctantly, Doc led the team back in the direction to change back into their original clothes, but they didn't make it that far.

18

KNIGHTS AGAINST PIRATES

During the trek back to the keep, Q lagged back a bit with Noah and Madeleine to thank them for their help in the search: Noah, for his knowledge of Templar beliefs and practices; Madeleine for her painstaking research that led to the treasure, and for her compassion and tact in handling interactions with the guardian knight (which officially never happened).

Q stopped them momentarily to acknowledge, "Without the two of you, what we accomplished here today wouldn't have been possible. And while I must stress that it hasn't yet been scientifically verified that the pyramid we found does, in fact, contain the lost treasure of the Knights Templar, I'm appreciative and proud to have served with the two of you.

"Thank you both on behalf of the President of the United States and the nation."

"Can you put that in writing?" asked Doc, half in jest.

"Most of it," Q replied, with a broad grin.

"We found it, Q! We actually found it!" Madeleine could hardly contain herself.

"Well, remember what I just said, Madeleine," Q replied. "We don't yet know for sure what we've found. The Navy is about to secure this site, and Pentagon analysts will do their thing over the next couple of weeks."

"That's your reality, Marshal," she giggled. "My reality is that I've finally validated years of research. The years of withering criticism from scoffers who ridiculed me privately and publicly are over. Say what you must officially, Q. I know in my heart we've found the lost treasure of the Knights Templar."

While Madeleine, Noah, and Q were having their conversation, Mountain took advantage of the quiet moment to speak his mind and heart to Doc.

"It's great serving with you again, Doc," Mountain said. "I'm sorry I ever doubted you and I hope you know how much it means to complete another mission with you."

"The feeling is mutual, Mountain," Doc told him. "Today has erased the years of worry and doubt we suffered since we served together in uniform. Thank you, Mountain, for being my brother-in-arms."

"There you are, Mountain," an unfamiliar voice interrupted Doc.

The voice belonged to a powerfully built, dark-skinned brute in a suit, with an AK-47 slung over one shoulder. With him were three others dressed and armed the same way.

"We've been looking everywhere for you, Mountain. Thanks for leaving the SUV parked outside. We never would've guessed you'd still be here at such a late hour if we hadn't seen it in the parking lot. Please introduce us to your friend. Or better yet, let me guess. Could he be Captain John Holiday, who once took a bullet meant for the President of the United States?"

"My friends call me Doc," Doc confirmed calmly. "But please don't. And let me guess, you actually tell people you're a Somali businessman with holdings in international shipping."

"Well, Mr. Holiday," the pirate replied, "I see that you're not only well-dressed and well-spoken, you're also a man of great wit. Those are all admirable qualities."

"You should practice what you preach," Doc shot back.

"Doc's my good friend, Jappa," Mountain said. "I won't let you hurt him!"

"There's no need for anyone to get hurt, Mountain," Jappa clarified, "so long as we all understand that the so-called hidden treasure of the Knights Templar belongs to us now."

"Really?!" Doc feigned astonishment. "You found it?! Congratulations! Where is it?"

"Enough with the foolish talk!" Jappa shouted. "The treasure now belongs to us!"

"If you'd like, we'd be happy to help you load it into your vehicle," Doc offered.

Noah, Madeleine, and Q caught up to Doc and the others and knew immediately they'd missed an important part of the conversation.

"What's up?" Q asked, hoping to break the tension he sensed.

"Jappa here seems to think his team's found the lost treasure of the Knights Templar. Isn't that amazing news?! You have alerted the Knights Templar haven't you?" he asked Jappa. "I'm sure they'd love to know their carelessness has been rectified. They've probably been worried sick the past 700 years."

"Stop this foolishness!" Jappa shouted and pointed his AK-47 at the team. "Put your hands in the air and make your way out of the fortress. We've a vehicle waiting to take you to safety, where you will be treated fairly until your President tells us what we should do with you. I hope for your sake he's a reasonable man. In your case, Captain Holiday, I should think he may even be persuaded to cover the added costs of your shipping and handling."

Doc understandably had no intention to cooperate with Jappa and his brutes. The former SEAL knew the situation called for immediate action. So, he was thrilled that Q had a semi-automatic Kriss Vector II under his tunic. When Doc watched Q tape the compact 9mm pistol to his stomach back in the keep, he thought it must be an uncomfortable way to conceal and carry a weapon. But Doc found it very comforting that Q had chosen a 30-round clip and that he had quickly moved into firing position in front of the team.

The pirates laughed when they saw Doc kneel and make the sign of the cross. They laughed even harder when Noah, Mountain, and Madeleine did the same. But they stopped laughing when Q opened fire and mowed them down. Mountain and Doc pulled their weapons in the chaos Q created. Doc needed just one shot to drop one of

Jappa's brutes who stood up to fire. But as Doc fired that round, he failed to see Jappa aim a pistol at him. Mountain saw it and jumped in front of Doc, taking a 45mm bullet to the heart. As Mountain fell, Doc emptied his nine-round clip into the pirate.

"MOUNTAIN!' Madeleine screamed.

She knelt beside the mighty Samoan and cried out, "Please God, NO! Please God NO!" over and over.

Doc started CPR immediately but the good Lord already had Mountain with him. While Doc worked frantically, SEAL Team Warriors charged up the Templar tunnel from their landing craft in the harbor. They would have arrived sooner, but it took longer than they had hoped to subdue the 33 pirates who had tried to stop them.

Grady and Grump helped Doc to his feet.

"We've got ya, Doc," Grady said.

"It's great to see ya', Doc," Grump added. "Thank God you're okay!"

Thunder One and Thunder Two lifted Mountain's heroic, lifeless body onto a stretcher and ran back to their landing craft.

Madeleine, Noah, Q, and Doc walked across the star-lit sand to the boat and held onto Mountain's body on the trip to the waiting carrier. Doc couldn't help but wonder what the crew must have thought as they watched SEAL Team Warriors escort the Knights Templar aboard.

Later that night, Q found Doc at the railing outside the bridge, staring back in the direction of Israel.

"What are you thinking?" he asked his friend.

"I forgot my cane," Doc murmured sadly. "I left it in the keep when we changed."

"It'll keep," Q said, hoping to make Doc smile. And it did.

Thirty hours later, Doc and Q told the entire story to the President in the Oval Office.

"What the two of you've accomplished for our nation is incredible!" the President praised. "It's absolutely INCREDIBLE! We and the other NATO members chased Jappa and his bunch for more than 12 years to bring them to justice. You've wiped that mission off the books. The other matter is one I hope you can understand I can't discuss. However, I can tell you, that I'll announce to the nation this evening that the United States is proud to have formally signed on to a historic and potentially lucrative partnership with six private American corporations, each of which has committed vast sums of money to advance our national security and prosperity through the exploration and economization of outer space."

With that, the President jumped up from his chair, ran around President Reagan's executive desk, and vigorously shook the hands of both men.

"You both did a FANTASTIC job! I thank you fellas from the bottom of my heart. And to show my appreciation, I've authorized time and funding for you both—and your significant others, of course—to enjoy a month at the destination of your choice, as a token of the appreciation and thanks from the citizens of the United States.

"Q, I would appreciate meeting briefly with you here again at 1900 this evening to discuss your next assignment," the President said. Then the President leaned against the "Resolute" desk—which had formerly been leaned on by Presidents Kennedy, Carter, Reagan, Clinton, Bush "43", and Obama—and he said, "Doc, I expect you back here at 0630 tomorrow morning, at which time I'll renew my offer to you to become my Senior Advisor For Military Affairs. And don't bother shaking your head now. I happen to know your physical limitations are a thing of the past…and judging by your recent performance, it's clear you have no significant intellectual limitations. So take all the time you need over the next few hours to think it over and we'll discuss your decision in the morning, when your head has cleared.

"So, unless you have any substantive questions you believe I might be able to answer, I thank you both again and will see you soon."

With that, Doc and Q exited the Oval Office and headed out the North Entrance of the White House for a walk in Lafayette Square, to answer a few of each other's questions.

"Okay, Doc," Q started cheerfully, "what do you want to know?"

"Well, for starters, how did you know so much about the coins I dug out of that mound in Acre?" Doc asked.

"Aha! This may surprise you, but I wasn't always a U.S. Marshal," Q confessed with a chuckle.

"So you're going to tell me you once were a coin dealer?" Doc assumed.

Q laughed and explained. "I once specialized in numismatics in the Secret Service."

"The study of the collection of coins, tokens, paper money,

and related objects," Doc pulled from the recesses of his memory.

"Roger that!" Q answered. "And verrrrrry good, for an old seadog. Keep this up, and you'll have me believing you were once a pirate yourself."

"I'm more than a pretty face," Doc laughed in response. "So, you were telling me the truth about those coins?" he asked.

"You're fixated on those coins, aren't you?" Q chuckled.

"It's just that I have a hard time getting my head around the idea that the bag I dug up contained coins worth $25 million," Doc explained.

"Well, it's the truth, Doc," Q stated. "Every word of it… and every penny."

"And no government has a legal claim to any of the treasure?" Doc asked.

"I'm not a lawyer, Doc, but I've been told that by lawyers," Q answered.

"So what happened to it?" Doc wondered out loud.

"We'll never know, Doc," Q answered. "And I believe that's far better than knowing."

"Why do you say that?" Doc asked.

"With so much money," Q said. "With even a tenth of that much money, you can bet you'd have issues with what happens to at least some of it."

"Excellent point," Doc conceded.

"Your turn," Doc told Q.

"Why did you turn down the President's original offer to be his Senior Advisor for Military Affairs?" Q asked. "That job will establish you as a significant, powerful source on the international stage long after you leave the position: Book deals, more speaking engagements than you'd have time for, probably a couple of honorary doctorates from the world's most prestigious universities, and last, but by no means least, your choice of several plum corporate board seats. Are you out of your ever-loving mind?"

"I know you're sick of hearing this, Q," Doc suggested, "but you know it's true: Washington is a swamp. I've always disliked the idea of getting stabbed in the back, and the way I see it, it's far more likely to happen to me in D.C. than anywhere else in the world. You know what I mean?"

"I do, Doc," Q conceded. "I truly do."

"So I'm not at all sure how I'm going to approach tomorrow's meeting with the President. But I've got another meeting here in the neighborhood to talk with another man about a horse in about an hour. He's not going to be too happy with me either, I think."

"You do have a way of irritating people, Doc," Q chuckled. "I'll be anxious to hear how it works out. But hey, before you go, Marsha asked me to be sure to ask you if you've spoken to Connie lately."

"I didn't know this was going to get personal," Doc half joked.

"Well then, forget I asked," Q said.

"No, it's okay, Q," Doc assured him. "I'm kinda' glad you asked."

"Why's that?" Q wondered.

"I need the push it's going to take to reach out and admit that I should've been more open to what was happening between us. My mind was so locked into sorting out what the world and the future held for 'ME' that I didn't have the time and energy needed to explore just how big a part of my world and my future Connie could become."

"So do you plan to try to do anything to fix that," Q asked, "or are you going to spend the rest of your miserable life regretting it?"

"What do you care?" Doc asked half in jest.

"I care, Doc," Q told him. "The work we do is so real: no one wants to know about it…and no one we love can know about it. But it's work that must get done, and it's wiser and safer to have men like you and me doing it for the right reasons, than to have others doing it for the wrong reasons. And the cost of having men like you do it is high enough, without it also costing you whatever genuine happiness you happen to find in this world."

"That was pretty good, Q," Doc said. "Did you read that somewhere, or did it come right off the top of your head?"

"Knock it off, Doc," Q shot back. "I'm being real with you, chump."

"I know, Q, and I appreciate it," Doc admitted. "Without having you to express it that way to me, I just might have pushed it all to the back of my mind and sabotaged things with Connie."

"S'okay, Doc," Q said and gave Doc a fist-bump. "No charge…and you're welcome!"

Doc took a leisurely route on his walk to St. John's. He dodged rush-hour traffic to cross H Street and grab a

"Post" from the box to see what the latest spin was on the President. Dodging his way back across the street to the church, Doc remembered how painful the walk was for him the last time.

This visit, Doc led himself into the small library behind the altar, opened the huge, leather-bound book still in place on the pedestal, and inserted his Trident into the cut-out pages. The hidden door opened and Doc entered Keeper's unique meeting room for high-stakes contractors like Doc. Doc took his usual seat, but occupied it in a much more relaxed position than he did for his first visit. Keeper entered precisely on time, very well-dressed and looking refreshed and happy as he sat in the oversized high-back chair behind a large desk.

"Hello, Doc!" Keeper proclaimed to him as he entered. "It's good to see you looking so healthy. How are you feeling? How's the pelvis? Man oh man, you hit it out of the park for me, Doc. I can't thank you enough…and remember I warned you when you see your check," he said with a stilted chuckle.

"I'm feeling terrific, sir," Doc said. "Thanks for askin'. Judging by your exuberance, I'm guessing that the 'items' we secured were the ones you hoped for, and their estimated value is at least in the neighborhood you anticipated."

"Unfortunately, I'm not at liberty to even discuss the particulars of your mission, Doc," Keeper replied, a bit disingenuously. "However, I'm thrilled to report that subsequent to events while you were away, our organization has secured significant funding originating from an extremely diverse amalgamation of anonymous sources throughout Europe, the Middle East, and even parts of Asia. In short, we're currently positioned to be the world leader in space exploration and economization through this century."

"Keeper, you used a whole lot of syllables just to tell me you've got enough money to go to the moon, Mars, and God only knows where else," Doc said. "I'm happy to see you so happy. I'll consider the mission a success."

"That's putting it much too mildly, Doc," Keeper confirmed. "But it's best if we just leave it at that for now. Being a strategic thinker, I'd like to discuss a career opportunity with you before I present you with your check for payment in full for this first mission.

"Doc, I'm hoping you'll join my organization as an Executive Vice President and my Chief Security Officer. Our business interests have a worldwide reach. And thanks to your impressive efforts those interests will soon be interplanetary. By the time you achieve retirement age, our reach may well be intergalactic. You've played a major role in making it all possible. It goes without saying that this organization will continue to thrive with the help of your knowledge, skills, talent, and wisdom. I'm prepared to make you the highest-paid senior executive in the entire aero-space industry, as well as award you with a significant financial interest that will continue to reward you—and quite frankly your descendants—in the century ahead. Can I welcome you aboard, Doc?"

"Whew, Keeper," Doc professed, and ran a hand through his hair. "If my sense of humor was still as corny as it once was, I'd asked you to run that all by me one more time. But there's really no need for that. Frankly, despite my greatly improved physical condition, this last mission took its toll on me emotionally. I lost a very good friend, and no amount of success is worth that cost. It'll be quite some time before I'm able to focus much attention on things like career and financial rewards."

"I certainly can respect that, Doc," Keeper replied as he plucked a check out of what looked like a gigantic ledger. "And on that note, I'm pleased to present you with this check in appreciation for your service and performance."

Doc walked briskly to Keeper's desk, reached over, and took the check. Doc went dead silent when he read *One Billion Dollars*. It took Doc a few moments to gather himself before he felt comfortable speaking.

"Um…Keeper, this isn't even funny," Doc's voice almost broke before he choked out the words. "What I did doesn't warrant this amount of money."

"To be completely honest with you, Doc," Keeper alleged, "I'm happy to hear you say that, because I had to justify giving you what is clearly a significantly smaller fee than my Board of Directors had authorized me to pay you."

"They wanted to pay me more?!" Doc somehow managed to verbalize.

"Significantly more," Keeper clarified. "But I convinced them that the reduced amount was more than fair…and that I could've paid you far less, in light of your breach of our contract."

"What on earth are you talking about?" Doc said with a sense of insult.

"You essentially entered into a joint venture with a competitor, a move explicitly prohibited by the contract you accepted and signed, potentially putting the interests of you and your collaborative partner ahead of those of my organization. In short, Doc, you ran around playing knights and pirates on my dime, with a former colleague, who was employed by an entity whose interests are in direct conflict with mine. On a bad day, I'd tell you to get out of my office and sue me before I'd pay you a penny."

"Do you really have that much hate bottled up inside you?!" Doc asked in amazement. "For the record, I would've been happy to walk out of here with my pelvis, my back, and my dignity all intact. But since the money is on the table, I'll take it. As for the job offer: No thanks!

"And for the record, that 'former colleague' of mine, whose interests you think were in conflict with yours, saved my life...and perhaps the mission as well. You and I will never know for sure. All I do know is that my friend gave his life for me, and you and I are walking around rich thanks to him. So I'll cash this check, Keeper. You're damn right, I will. And I'll do my best to use the money in ways that would make him happy, proud, and thankful. I'd advise you to do the same. His name was Kenesaw Mountain Matua, but we just called him Mountain. He loved this country that just made me very rich, and made you even richer. And if you'd ever care to know more about him, give me a call!"

Doc was grateful he could again take long walks. The next morning he walked for several miles before he had to hail a cab to the White House for his meeting with the President. He figured it was time to talk openly with the President about working for Keeper, since he obviously already knew most of the details.

"The man is certainly successful and he pays very well, but he's an absolute jerk," he told the President.

"Don't be too hard on him, Doc," the President cautioned. "It's been a nightmare year for the man. It really has."

"Yeah, it must be a terrible nightmare to have to split $400 billion," Doc said sarcastically.

"He couldn't care less about the money, Doc. It's just a means to an end for him," the President added. "It nearly crushed him when his wife committed suicide. And then his brother's breakdown nearly caused an international incident."

"What did his brother do?" Doc asked.

"Nothing, thanks to you and your team," the President answered.

"Wait a minute!" Doc barked. "Captain Augustus Baird is Keeper's brother?"

"Of course. I thought you knew," the President admitted, matter-of-factly.

"So what's Keeper's real name?" Doc asked in disbelief.

"Jonah Baird, he's the billionaire CEO of his aero-space brainchild, Dark Yonder, Doc. You didn't even know his name or any of this the whole time you were working for him? I wondered why you insisted on calling him Keeper."

"He insisted on it," Doc said, more than a little embarrassed…and repentant.

"It was a fitting code name. He's definitely his brother's keeper. Your rescue of his brother served as a resume to him," the President added. "He was in the Oval Office that afternoon, going on and on about what an incredible job you and your team did on the *Reagan*, and how very grateful he was that his brother—and the nation—were safe."

"He knew all about that?!" Doc asked in utter amazement.

"He helped plan and fund it," President Preston maintained. "He came to me asking permission to send a private team of contractors in and snatch his brother off the carrier. I told him we had a better option. And you guys pulled it off, such a beautiful job I wish I could brag about it.

"He called me last night after you turned his job offer down," the President told Doc.

"Yeah, well you could say we didn't hit it off," Doc said, almost apologetically.

"Don't let it bother you, Doc. I think he ultimately was glad you turned him down. My guess is that he offered it out of a sense of obligation and appreciation. He adores his older brother. And frankly, you pulled the good Captain's ass out of the fire, along with our national security. I'll say it one more time, Doc. Your team did an amazing job that day. We averted what could've been a terrifying international incident with China, and your men didn't so much as scratch the paint on the *Reagan*. You shook its crew to their core. But they'll eventually get over it. They may even figure out what happened," the President said with a hearty laugh.

"The nation needs more good men like you and your team, Doc," President Preston suggested.

"If you ever need me, Mr. President, I'm just a phone call away," Doc promised.

"So you're turning my job offer down again," the President

sighed. "I just can't seem to talk you into punching a clock here every day," he told Doc and laughed some more.

"I do have a favor to ask of you, Mr. President," Doc inquired tentatively.

"I lost one of my best men, Kenesaw Mountain Matua, in Israel during the Templar mission. He was the best of us, Mr. President, a courageous warrior, who gave his life for his country. He deserves a hero's resting place. He has no family, so I'm hoping to bury him in Arlington."

"Done!" the President confirmed powerfully. "I'll have his paperwork on my desk today and someone will call you within 24 hours to make it happen. You're a great leader, Doc. Your men were lucky to have you. Bravo!"

"Thanks again, Mr. President," Doc acknowledged one more time.

"It's my pleasure, believe me, Doc," the President said. "Take care and God bless!"

19

ROOM 7

The following day, Connie was rushing to an impromptu meeting when she passed by what she thought was an unoccupied room in ICU. Next, the corner of her eye caught a glimpse of what looked like a heavily bandaged adult patient in dual leg traction. Surprised that she didn't know about the patient beforehand, she waltzed straight to the nurses' station to learn what she could.

"Excuse me, Jan, but what do we know about the new patient in Room 7?" she asked.

"Room 7?" Jan replied. "There shouldn't be anyone in that room. It's been unavailable for the past two weeks because of renovations."

"That's what I thought," Connie admitted. "But there's someone in there right now. I just saw the patient with my own eyes. I really have to get to a scheduling meeting on the sixth floor. That'll take at least an hour, but I'd appreciate it if you'd please try to find out what you can while I'm gone."

"I'll do my best, Connie," Jan promised. "Good luck at your meeting."

"Thanks again!" Connie said and headed to her meeting.

Connie was back at the nurses' station just before lunch for an update on the patient.

"Sorry, Connie," Jan apologized. "But I haven't been able to learn a thing about him."

"Well, that's strange," Connie murmured with a wrinkled brow. "We've no insurance data?"

"Nope," Jan remarked. "He's a self-funded, private payer."

"Well, we know he's filthy rich!" Connie proclaimed. "Get a priest down here, and I'll have him perform a wedding."

"I couldn't even find a spouse or relative in the files for the patient," Jan alleged, still staring at her computer monitor. "In fact, the patient is so heavily bandaged, I couldn't tell if it's a male or a female. Considering size and weight, I'd say it's a male."

"Are we even sure it's human…and alive?!" Connie asked, to magnify the absurdity of it all.

"I take it there's not so much as a chart at the end of the bed?" Connie inquired.

"Nada!" Jan shrugged and moved on to the next records request in her stack.

Connie did her best to be cheerful and positive as she entered Room 7.

"Good afternoon!" she announced with her beaming smile. "My name's Connie, and I'm your duty nurse for the day. Can you speak without too much difficulty?"

"Uuuuhhhh…" Connie heard escape the patient's bandaged face.

"Can you tell me your name?" Connie asked. "How about your doctor's name?"

"Uuuuhhhh…" the patient grunted again.

"Can you tell me why you're here?" Connie attempted one last question.

"Uhh UHHH!" The patient seemed to make a real effort with that answer.

"What did you say?" Connie questioned again, moving to the bedside.

"Uhh UHHH!" the patient grunted again, more forcefully.

Connie couldn't see anything but the patient's eyes, due to the heavy bandaging. She thought she'd try carefully removing some of the bandages around the patient's mouth and jaw, which might make it easier for the patient to speak and be understood. So she carefully snipped away some of the bandages using her surgical scissors. One snip at a time, she gently freed the patient's jaw and lips. Then she asked again.

"Now, can you please try again to tell me why you're here?" Connie probed on last time.

"I…I…I fell," the patient said, clearly.

"You fell?" Connie echoed the patient in surprise.

She was more than surprised to see such extensive injuries sustained in a fall, unless it was a fall from a tall building.

"Can you tell me where you fell?" she tried a second question.

"Here," the patient said, weakly.

"What's that?" Connie was sure she hadn't heard the patient correctly.

"H…Here. I fell herrrrrre," the patient struggled, but got it out clearly.

"How long ago did you fall here?" Connie felt the answer to this question should be enough to at least finally identify the patient.

"Four…four…four months ago," the patient managed to answer.

"Four months ago!" repeated loudly. "That's impossible!" she reiterated. "That's absolutely impossible," she insisted. "Where have you been all this time?"

"Uhh…" The patient had reverted to mumbling.

Totally frustrated by the agonizing pace of extracting the information she needed so badly, Connie then ran to the nurses' station and grabbed a small white board and a marker and ran back into Room 7. She gently put the marker in the patient's right hand and held the white board to enable the patient to answer her questions.

"Now," she advised softly to the patient.

"When did you fall here at the hospital?" she asked again.

Four months ago, the patient clearly wrote.

Dumbfounded, Connie asked, "How did you fall?"

In love, the patient clearly wrote.

"No." Connie was sure the patient hadn't heard her. "HOW did you fall?"

Finally, the patient took a deep breath and wrote a full sentence.

I fell in love here four months ago! the white board read.

Connie studied the message, and then looked at the patient's eyes. They were clearly a man's eyes...and they were beginning to tear up.

"Doc?" Connie almost whispered. "Doc, is it you?" she asked plainly.

The patient began bouncing and rolling from side to side...and laughing. The sight shocked and confused Connie. The whole experience shook her staid approach to relating to hurting patients.

"Connie! Get me out of these bandages before I wet my pants!" the patient managed to say while laughing hysterically. Connie was positive the patient sounded like Doc, but this was just too crazy a stunt for the "Doc" she knew. But her gut told her it was Doc. Connie began cutting the bandages off as fast as she carefully could, beginning around the mouth and jawline.

"You're beautiful, and you're very good with surgical scissors," Doc professed between bursts of laughter. "I believe you've a future in nursing."

"John Henry Holiday, I can't believe you would pull a stunt like that!" Connie almost shouted at him. "And you did it at my workplace! What's wrong with you?"

"I told you, Connie," Doc confessed seriously. "I fell in love here four months ago. It might have actually been during my very first visit here. But I'm not sure I'd admit that if I knew it."

"So there's nothing physically wrong with you?" she asked, just to be sure. "You're okay? This is just a stupid stunt? Doc, you're an idiot! This is a hospital ICU for God's sake. You're in a bed that someone else could be waiting for! Didn't you think about that?"

"I thought about it, Connie," Doc maintained seriously, still gently pulling tape off of himself. "I've given it an awful lot of thought. That's why I made a donation to the hospital this morning. When the CEO asked me what he could do to thank me, I suggested he help me with this crazy scheme. He thought it would be a hoot...but I wouldn't give him permission to videotape it.

"Connie, I'm serious," Doc asserted softly, looking straight into her eyes. "I fell deeply in love with you here at the hospital, and at the White House, and everywhere in between. Nothing in my life makes nearly as much sense without you in it. I want you in my life, Connie. I want to be in your life. I can't say that I'm smarter for having made the mistake of keeping my distance, but I know I'm wiser.

"Please give me another chance to show you how much you mean to me, and how much I can mean to you," Doc asked sincerely. "Please say you will."

Connie hugged Doc's neck so tightly she hurt a muscle on his right side. But there was no way he was going to interrupt the hug.

"Oh, Doc," she whispered through tears of joy and relief, "I've missed you so much! I've prayed night and day that you were missing me just as much. Another chance isn't needed, Doc. We had 'a moment' and now we're moving forward again…together."

"I love you Connie Walters," Doc said loud and clear, "and I certainly missed you night and day."

Doc checked his watch and realized he'd be late for a meeting if he didn't leave soon.

"I'm sorry, Connie, but I promised to meet Q to help him pick something out for his wife," he declared, as he paused halfway out the door of Room 7.

"It's okay, hon," Connie said for the first time. "I'm at work, remember? Can we meet for supper somewhere?"

"Sure we can!" Doc said with a beaming smile. "I'll pick a place and text you. See you at dinner! I love you, babe!"

"Love you too!" Connie replied as they headed in different directions…for a little while.

About the time Doc stepped onto the "Down" elevator on his way out, Connie was again rushing by the nurses' station, when Jan stopped her in her tracks.

"Connie! Oh, Connie!" Jan squealed and waved her arms to attract attention.

"What is it, Jan?" Connie asked.

"Do you remember that Navy SEAL patient here about four months ago with a gunshot wound to the spine?" Jan asked excitedly.

"Why, uhh, yes, I believe I remember him." Connie had just hugged and kissed him!

"Doris from accounting just called me, and guess what?!" Jan was absolutely bursting to tell what she knew.

"I'm not a good guesser, Jan," she said. "So please just tell me."

"He just donated ten million dollars to the hospital!" she squealed. "Can you believe it?! I didn't think Navy SEALS were paid so well."

"Ten million dollars?" Connie repeated in disbelief. "Captain John Henry Holiday donated $10 million to the hospital?"

"You remember him that well, do you?" Jan asked in surprise. "Did you know he had that kind of money?"

"Yes, I recall him very well," Connie confirmed. "But no, I had no idea he had that kind of money. I'm thrilled to hear the news though, and I'm eager to hear the details."

Of course, Connie was sure she'd hear the details that evening.

It's going to be a very interesting supper! Connie thought on her way to the last meeting of the day.

Supper was at The Lafayette on 16th Street NW. Doc called Connie to let her know he was sending a car for her. She felt rushed to prepare for the five-star restaurant, but was excited to experience it. Doc was too. After all, he could afford it now.

"Hi, Doc!" Connie said as she kissed him lightly and slid in next to him in the booth. "You've got a whole lot to tell me, don't you? At least, that's what everyone at the hospital says. So eat and drink to your heart's content…and spill your guts about where all this sudden money is coming from. Not that I mind, mind you!" she accentuated with her wonderful laugh.

"Well, I must tell you that, yes, it's an interesting story. But I lost a very dear friend as it unfolded. I've arranged for him to be buried in Arlington Cemetery next week with full military honors. This mission took his life, but it also enabled me to honor that life in the way that he deserved. It couldn't have happened otherwise. His name was Kenesaw Mountain Matua, who lived up to his name. I'll tell you more about him most every time he comes to mind. But for now, just remember that without his help and sacrifice on this past mission, I might not only not be sitting here with you, I might well be the one scheduled for burial next week instead of him."

"I'm very, very sorry to hear about your friend," Connie asserted, "I truly am. And I look forward to hearing more and more about him. I've never met him, but I literally feel I owe my life to him," she said, and covered Doc's hands with hers.

"Thanks, baby!" he told her as the waiter arrived. "I'm starving!" Doc yelled way too loudly.

"Me too!" Connie announced even louder, and they both had a good laugh. "By the way, Doc, and forgive me for asking, but can you afford this place?"

"Honey," Doc whispered to her cheek-to-cheek, "believe me when I tell you that you'll never have to ask me that again."

Connie sat back in her chair, blinked several big blinks, and agreed, "Well, okay then!" and their laughter rang throughout the restaurant.

Supper in a public place gave Doc the luxury of avoiding discussion about his work—and exactly how much money he'd recently earned—in favor of small talk and big dreams with Connie. They were at her place by 8:00 o'clock and Doc recalled as much about the mission as Connie could absorb before having to get to sleep. She had to work in the morning. Doc, on the other hand, was sure the adrenalin he was running on would still be driving him in the morning. So he took a long shower, shaved, and climbed into bed with a book he bought on the way home. It was a novel he'd always promised himself he would read: *Ben Hur: A Tale of the Christ*. And finally, he was going to begin.

As Doc read the opening pages, Connie was hurriedly completing her work-night routine. Once she finally settled into bed, her mind eventually came to rest thinking about one of the first things Doc said to her that she just knew she'd never forget: "Everything happens for a reason." She reached for the small bottle of moisturizer on her night-stand and slowly and gently worked it into her hands, arms, neck, and face. As she did, she let her mind run through a short list of recent occurrences that were seemingly unrelated as they happened, but ultimately shared a clearly interdependent relevance.

Could it really be true? she wondered. *How strange it was*, she thought in that moment, *to have traveled so far into adulthood and still be unsure of how life really unfolds. What is it about the contradictions of interwoven causes versus purely random occurrences that haunt us throughout our lives?* she thought. *Why will they not leave us alone? Why must we literally command ourselves to believe one or the other in order to have any hope of banishing the chaos their coexistence brings? Most importantly, if the universe truly is a godless, mindless, random place, why does Doc's belief have so many propo-nents with life-changing testimonies?*

"Questions like that are far too big and heavy to bring to bed on a work-night," Connie told herself as she returned the moisturizer to her nightstand and turned off the lamp.

She awoke an hour early the next morning to the sound of Doc ringing her doorbell.

"Doc?" she asked through blurry eyes. "What are you doing here? What time is it?"

"It's almost 6 o'clock, babe," Doc confirmed excitedly. "Sorry if I'm interrupting you when you're getting ready for work, but I just had to talk to you about something important, and it can't wait until you get off work."

"The only thing you interrupted was my sleep, Doc," she answered groggily. "This better be really important."

"Oh it is, babe," he proclaimed excitedly. "It really is and I've got to get your answer so we can discuss something else I didn't tell you at supper last night."

"Well, come on and make yourself at home. I've got to get ready for work now that you've started my day for me. And you've got to start the coffee, eggs, bacon, and toast. I like my coffee black, my eggs scrambled, my bacon extra crispy, and my toast not too dark."

"I can do that, hon!" he assured her confidently and turned to head to the kitchen.

"Whoa!" Connie said and grabbed hold of the sleeve of Doc's jacket. "Before anything else, at least tell me what the really important thing is you need to talk to me about, so I don't spend my entire shower wondering about it."

"I…I… Well, I…" Doc stammered.

"Would you please just spit it out, so I can get into a hot shower? I'm freezing, Doc!" she grumbled.

"Connie, I love you deeply, more than life itself, and I'd be the happiest man in the world if you'll marry me," Doc blurted out in a single breath.

Connie was stunned. It was the question she'd hoped for since Doc stopped calling months before.

"Yes! Yes, Doc!" she confirmed excitedly, then pulled him over by his sleeve. "Forget breakfast!" she said, then kissed him passionately and led him into the shower before he could even get his clothes off.

When the shower had come to a glorious end and Connie was happily dressing for work, Doc called Q to let him on the wedding plans.

"Q, will you be my best man?" he asked.

"Of course!" Q happily agreed. "Man, the wife's going to be thrilled to hear the news. She predicted this would happen since I first told her about you and Connie."

"By the way, Q," Doc said apologetically, "I don't even know your wife's name."

"Marsha," Q said.

"So you're Marshal Marshall, and you're wife's name is Marsha Marshall?"

"That's not funny, Doc," Q said, obviously tired of having it emphasized.

"No, it's not funny," Doc agreed, "but ya gotta admit it's easy to remember!"

20

THE DIFFERENCE

Connie and Doc enjoyed the warm early afternoon sun on their patio, overlooking Flathead Lake, and watched for the seaplane that was bringing Q and Marsha from Spokane. The sky was a beautiful deep blue and held the promise of a classic Washington sunset.

The patio looked south, toward Wild Horse Island, and was the perfect spot to watch the seaplane land and pull alongside their dock below. While they waited for the plane's arrival, they shared a glass of the fresh apple juice Connie bought at the farmers' market the day before.

Earlier that afternoon, Doc helped Connie prep the roast that was filling the first floor with an aroma that would welcome their good friends and make them want to stay. When the plane finally arrived, they watched Q and Marsha climb out and slip into the SUV Doc had parked there for them that morning with the key under the mat. The lake was still a place where you could do that without a second thought, which is one of the reasons why Connie and Doc decided to make it their home.

"Come help me make the salad," Connie insisted, grabbing Doc's hand

"It'll be great to spend time with them again," Doc remarked as he chopped the carrots.

"Yes, it will," Connie agreed. "And we'll have all day tomorrow and half of the next day to catch up on things before Madeleine and Noah arrive. I'm so glad everyone had the time available to make this happen," she exclaimed. "I can hardly wait for Monday evening and supper with all four of them. I'm so excited about our surprise for them!"

Everything was perfect, especially Q and Marsha being able to enjoy a week's stay and help celebrate Madeleine and Noah's marriage. And Q's knock on the front door, set everything in motion.

"HELLO!" he and Marsha shouted in unison when Connie opened the door with Doc standing close behind her. Connie knew Marsha was a hugger and gave her a long, tight squeeze to make sure she knew how much she'd missed her. Doc grabbed Q's hand and pulled him into a hug as well. The months had moved too slowly for friends that hated to be apart.

"It's great having you both here," Doc told them as he grabbed the two biggest suitcases and led the way to the bedroom they'd use for the week.

"It's perfect!" Marsha said as she took in the view from the large window across from the king bed.

"Happy wife, happy life!" Q maintained and flashed his bright, broad smile.

"Are you hungry?" Connie asked.

"I'm starving!" Marsha sighed, and followed her into the kitchen.

"We're right behind ya," Doc confirmed and made way for Q to fall in behind the women.

Over lunch, they talked about the hundreds of things, big and small, that had occurred since they were last together. The conversation continued unbroken throughout the afternoon and evening. After one of Connie's trademark Italian suppers, she took Marsha to her sewing room to show her the quilts she was working on, and the one she'd just completed and planned to give to Madeleine and Noah.

Doc and Q headed to the patio with a bottle of brandy and sat under the stars. The full moon was low in the sky and its light danced on the surface of the lake.

"This place is truly beautiful," Q contended quietly, then took his first sip of brandy and drew on his cigar.

Doc propped his feet up on the railing and it reminded him of times that now seemed so long ago, before he knew Q or Connie, and long before he'd ever heard of Flathead Lake or ever dreamed of living in such a place. Now, here he—and they—were.

God is truly good! he thought to himself.

Q propped his feet up next to Doc's.

"Marsha says I have big feet for a man my size," Q

mentioned and took another sip of brandy. "Do you think my feet are big, Doc?"

"I'm in no position to question Marsha's judgement, Q," Doc said slowly. "Although it's tempting sometimes. Look who she married, for instance."

"This is great brandy, Doc," Q said. "What kind is it?"

"Germain-Robin Select Barrel XO. It's a mouthful in more ways than one," Doc chuckled.

"The President sent it as a wedding gift."

"Must be expensive," Q guessed.

"Oh yeah!" Doc confirmed. "Believe me, it's good to be on his gift list."

"Speaking of gifts," Q confessed, "I've got something for you."

"Well, that sure wasn't necessary," Doc grunted over his shoulder as Q went for the gift.

The box Q brought to the patio could only contain one thing. But Doc held himself in check, hoping his guess was right and not wanting to be disappointed.

Doc carefully unwrapped the colorful paper. Since he was a kid, he'd had "a thing" about not wanting to tear the wrappings on his gifts. So Q was soon prodding him to "hurry up." Once Doc removed the wrapping, he lifted the top off the cardboard box inside. Inside that box, he found a beautiful, hand-carved mahogany box with a polished brass catch and hinges.

"Would you just hurry up and open it, please?!" Q groaned and bounced in his chair.

Doc finally did open it and was thrilled by the sight of a brand new mahogany cane, identical to the one he'd left in the Templar fortress in Acre. Much to Doc's amazement, it even had a new gold Trident inlaid in the handle, identical to the original.

"Where did you manage to get this?" he asked Q.

"Same place you got the brandy," Q said simply.

Q was thrilled to see the look in Doc's eyes as he hefted the cane and admired it from top to bottom. Doc ran his hand over the inlaid Trident, deeply admiring the workmanship.

"Give it a good going over, Doc," Q said. "Let me know if you see the difference."

"It's different?" Doc asked.

"Oh yeah! In a big way," Q replied.

The only difference Doc detected at first was the thin brass ring around the shaft at the base of the handle. He noticed what seemed to be a joint, as if the handle could be separated from the shaft. But pulling and twisting did no good.

"Push on the tip of the anchor with a finger, Doc," Q told him.

Doc pushed as directed and discovered the tip was spring-loaded.

"Now pull easy on the handle," Q said.

Doc pulled and felt the handle coming away from the shaft. With it, came a brilliantly polished, 40-inch, carbon steel blade, etched with the SEAL moto: *If knocked down, I'll get back up, every time.*

"Hoooooly cow!" Doc exclaimed in wonder. "It's beautiful!"

"I'm glad you like it, Doc," Q remarked happily. "I wasn't sure how you'd feel about it. But I figured if you're going to have it with you, and if you're going to continue to get into pinches, you just may be thankful you have it one day."

"I absolutely love it, Q!" Doc said. "You truly are a good friend."

"The best!" Q replied.

Doc kept the cane close the rest of the evening, often pulling the blade out, and putting it back in carefully.

"We've been through a lot in our short time together, haven't we Q?" Doc asked.

"Sure have," Q answered. "Some of it has even been enjoyable," he chuckled.

Doc poured more brandy for each of them and lit a cigar for himself.

"Your feet are kinda big, Q," Doc suggested quietly.

"My feet are not big!" Q refuted defensively.

"If you don't think your feet are big, why'd you ask?" Doc teased him.

"Because Marsha thinks they're big," Q answered.

"Do you believe everything she tells you?" Doc teased him some more.

"No, but I usually just agree with her," Q said shaking his head and smiling.

"That makes no sense," Doc suggested.

"Happy wife, happy life. That makes sense my good friend," Q advised and took another sip of brandy.

"Okay, so here's my big question for the night," Doc presented.

"Shoot!" Q confirmed.

"Remember that bit about the gold coins?" Doc asked.

"Yeah, what about it?" Q inquired.

"The President sent you on purpose, didn't he?" Doc questioned.

"Of course he sent me on purpose, Doc. What kind of question is that?" Q barked.

"No, I mean he sent you to Rome because he knew what I was looking for," Doc alleged.

"That's probably a safe assumption," Q agreed.

"There's a lot more going on in the Oval Office than we know isn't there?" Doc probed.

"That's also a safe assumption," Q agreed again.

"Do you want to take a ride to town with me in the morning?" Doc asked.

"Sure!" Q said and finished his brandy. "But I've had it for today, partner. I'm going to go find Marsha and head to the comfy bedroom you and Connie have put us up in. Goodnight."

"Goodnight, good friend," Doc stated and finished his brandy. "See you in the morning."

Q passed Connie on his way inside. She helped Doc to his feet and led him off to bed.

Doc was surprised to find her still awake when he finished his long shower and slipped under the covers.

"Thanks for the wonderful supper tonight, babe," he applauded. "It was wonderful."

"You helped," she reminded him.

"Yeah, I know," he revealed. "I peeled and chopped and tossed, but you put it all together, as you always do," he added as he rolled to face her, took her in his arms, and kissed her goodnight. He'd had too much brandy.

After a breakfast of Marsha's bacon biscuit breakfast bake, Q climbed into the SUV with Doc for the ride to town via the long route.

"What are we after?" Q asked.

"We've got quite a list, partner," Doc said. "We try to keep trips to town to a minimum."

"Can't say that I blame you," Q replied. "You've got a beautiful home, Doc."

"Glad you like it," Doc said simply.

"What's not to like?" Q noted.

"You and Marsha are welcome anytime you know," Doc reiterated genuinely

"And we appreciate it, Doc, we really do," Q remarked. "It's just hard getting away from work and all."

"I know what you mean, Q," Doc said. "Would you retire if you could?"

"In a heartbeat!" Q blurted out.

"Really?!" Doc said, a bit surprised. "Marsha, too?"

"That might be a different story," Q clarified. "She loves teaching."

"But she can do that anywhere, right?" Doc answered.

"Theoretically," Q partially agreed. "But Marsha's feelings about teaching are complicated."

"What women's feelings aren't complicated?!" Doc noted with a laugh. "But it sure would be swell to have you two close by all the time."

"We feel that way too, Doc," Q agreed. "But I sure don't see it in the cards right now."

"Cards can change, friend," Doc cited with a grin. "Cards can change."

In town, the guys started at the hardware store, looking at chainsaws, nail guns, drills, and at least a dozen other things Doc didn't really need. Next, it was the drugstore, bakery, and grocery store. Last stop was the gas station. Doc filled the tank while Q went inside to buy more cigars. He grabbed a soda and was standing in line to pay, but the guy in front of him was desperately asking the young cashier for directions.

"Where's Flat Head Lake?" he asked in a heavy Middle Eastern accent.

"You're there!" the high school-aged girl wearing a "Coco" ID badge said cheerfully.

"No! I'm not there! I cannot find the place I am looking

for!" he told her excitedly. "I'm sorry," he said. "But I'm frustrated. I have been looking all day."

"Do you have an address or a name of a town?" Coco asked.

"I lost the paper I wrote it on," he told her in frustration. "It's a very big house, right on the lake."

"I'm sorry sir," Coco conveyed, "but the lake is 27 miles long and 15 miles wide and there are lots of big homes on it. Do you have the name of the person you're looking for?"

Angry, exasperated, or just overwhelmed, the man stormed out of the store, leaving Coco out of sorts.

"I'm very sorry, sir," she apologized to Q.

"That's quite alright, miss," Q said. "I'm in no hurry. I don't know my way around here either, so I can relate to his frustration. It's a very big, very beautiful lake."

"We're pretty proud of it," Coco gushed.

When Q exited the station, he got a better look at the guy, who was standing outside his car in the sunlight. Q immediately received the familiar, nagging feeling that he'd seen the man before, but he felt nothing more specific.

"You look like you got a lot on your mind all of a sudden Q," Doc suggested when Q got in.

"Nothing important," Q said.

"That's not what your expression says," Doc pressed.

"I just saw a Middle Eastern fella in the gas station and I can't shake the feeling that I've seen him before," Q specified, still struggling to remember where he'd seen the man before.

"Well, let it go. You're on vacation," Doc reminded him.

"I know," Q admitted. "You're right, Doc. It's just that I'm usually so good with faces and I'm drawing a complete blank on this one. But if my mind is so blank, why am I so sure I've seen him before?"

"So is he a bad guy or a good guy?" Doc asked.

"I just don't know," Q answered.

"Well, taking my mind off of it usually helps for me," Doc told him. "Think about fishing, or boating, or hiking, or what you want for supper tonight. Get your mind off of it, and it'll eventually pop out of your brain when you least expect it."

"You're right, Doc," Q said. "You're absolutely right."

By the time they got back to the house, the wives were rushing around the house, getting it ready for Madeleine and Noah to arrive.

"I'm so excited to finally meet them in person!" Marsha gushed. "I've heard so much about the two of them. They seem like they're perfect for each other."

"I'm excited too!" Connie confirmed. "We've Skyped a number of times, but it's just not the same as meeting someone in person."

"Oh, I agree," Marsha said. "What time are you expecting them again?"

"Not really sure now," Connie stated in dismay. "The flight

was delayed in New York. Last time they called, they were still sitting around the airport waiting for a plane."

"That can be so frustrating!" Marsha admitted.

"I think I just heard Doc pull up," Connie mentioned. "They'll probably need help hauling the groceries into the house."

"I'm up for it!" Marsha said excitedly.

21

OLD HUNTING DOGS

C onnie could tell that Marsha was very happy to be with her and Doc again, which gave Connie a very good feeling. She and Doc were enjoying life to the fullest, thanks in large part to the amazing amount of money Doc earned on the Acre mission—but even more because of the good friends they met along the way. And Q and Marsha were among their very best.

Finished with errands, Doc and Q hopped back into the SUV for a trip around the lake. Small talk eventually gave way to bigger topics. The two men were roughly the same age, and their service to the nation to heart. They possessed an unfailing sense of right and wrong, and their word was their bond. Both were also familiar with adventure and danger and knew how to handle both. Yet, the two of them also had a soft side that always seemed to prevail. And most important to the President, they shared a passionate love of country.

Q and Doc had been fast friends since the day they met, and they'd continued to grow closer each day since. They both felt they had the President to thank for that. He'd put them together, and apparently found the partnership to his liking. Both men thought that was one of the President's greatest strengths. He seemed to have an innate ability to grasp what a man is all about after only a simple conversation or two. Sometimes, as in Doc's case, he saw it on paper before meeting him. Meeting Doc only confirmed what the President already highly suspected.

So when they talked about big questions, issues, and challenges, they were never surprised when they had very similar opinions and approaches. Their conversation during that long ride around the lake was no exception.

"Have you spoken to the President, Q?" Doc asked.

"Not recently," Q said. "You?"

"Nope," Doc said. "You know, the calm, quiet life is nice. It's real nice. But there are times when I miss the feeling that what I'm doing matters, that someone, usually someone I'll never meet, is counting on something to happen—or not happen—and I've got the responsibility to make it happen, or to stop it from happening.

"I get how average folks do important things that matter every day for themselves and their loved ones. I seriously get that," Doc explained. "But for me, the most fulfilling feeling is to help make the unseen things happen, things that average folks will never know about…but make real differences in matters of homeland security, foreign relations, and world peace."

"So are you worried that if you're not doing it, no one is?" Q probed.

"No, that's not it," Doc maintained.

"Are you worried that whoever's doing it can't do it as well as you?" Q pressed Doc.

"No, that's not it either," Doc assured him. "I guess you could say I just miss having a piece of the action."

"Oooooooh, I get it," Q exaggerated for effect.

"You get what?" Doc asked defensively.

"You're feeling like an old huntin' dog that ain't allowed in the back of the pickup truck no more."

Doc stared out the windshield without saying a word for a moment.

"Yeah," he finally confessed. "I guess that's a good way to describe it."

"Awwwoooooooo!" Q did his best to howl like and old hound dog.

"Awwwoooooooo!" they howled together and laughed hysterically.

"Damn! I'm just not ready to get old yet, Q," Doc suggested once they'd stopped laughing.

"Yeah, well you aren't they only hound dog who feels that way, Doc," Q said knowingly. "You can be sure of that, partner."

On the way around the lake, they passed through town and the gas station where Q saw the man he was sure he'd seen somewhere before.

"Have you figured out where you saw that hombre yet, Q?" Doc asked.

"Nope." Q said. "But I will. I don't get this kind of feeling about folks I just happen to run into twice in my life. My gut's telling me he's a bad dude."

"Well, I'll make you a deal," Doc proposed. "Noah and Madeleine are due in tomorrow afternoon. We'll help them get settled in, then enjoy a great supper, and catch up on the latest news in their lives. Afterward, if you still haven't remembered who our mystery man is, I'll crank up my computer and you can show me how you navigate the various federal data bases. If your stranger really is a bad guy, you'll find him. Deal?" Doc asked.

"Deal!" Q said and fist-bumped Doc.

Doc, Connie, Q, and Marsha were waiting at the dock when Madeleine and Noah's seaplane arrived. Doc could tell by the looks on their faces as they stepped from the plane to the dock that they were thrilled to be reunited with good friends. It made him happy because he and Q were so excited to finally introduce them to Connie and Marsha.

The six of them were definitely birds of a feather. And Doc was thrilled to have the opportunity—and the ability —to have them all gathered together. Madeleine's reaction was heartwarming as she rushed to the wives and embraced both of them at once. A casual observer would have thought the three of them were old friends. It made Doc, Q, and Noah laugh to see it.

"Oh my gosh! I'm so happy to finally meet you both!" Madeleine shouted as she hugged and was embraced back.

"Ladies," Doc announced when the hugs subsided, "I'm thrilled to introduce you to Madeleine and Noah Allaman! Madeleine, I'm pleased and honored to introduce you to my very beautiful and amazing wife, Constance—known far and wide as Connie."

"My turn to brag," Q jumped in to say. "Madeleine, I'm equally pleased and honored to introduce my stunning and sassy wife, Marsha."

"Welcome to both of you!" Connie shouted with open arms. "We're so excited to have you here to share our time and our home with you both."

"Believe me," Noah confirmed, "we're absolutely jazzed to be here with you. Washington is a ridiculously amazing place! And this lake is breathtaking from the air. What an incredible front yard you have!"

"We like it," Connie replied.

"Yeah, I don't have to mow it," Doc added and everyone laughed.

The group paused on the front porch of the house to take in the beauty of the last light of day painting the surface of the lake.

"Amazing!" Noah said and pulled Madeleine close.

"If you think that's amazing," Doc acknowledged, "wait until you taste the supper Connie and Marsha have prepared. I guarantee you'll say it's deliziosa!"

"Well, I can tell you it certainly smells deliziosa!" Madeleine said with a laugh.

Connie gave Doc several warm, happy glances during supper. He could tell she was pleased about the warmth and laughter everyone enjoyed around the table that evening.

"Time for dessert!" Connie announced when the supper plates stopped being passed.

"Who wants coffee?" Marsha asked and headed to the kitchen with Connie.

"I don't want to be left out," Madeleine stated with a smile as she stood to follow Marsha. "Besides, I'm dying to get a look at the kitchen."

"Well, Noah," Doc suggested with a smile when the men were alone, "if Q and I have taught you anything it's obviously how to marry a good and beautiful woman."

"And I appreciate it very much," Noah said as the three good friends chuckled.

Connie served homemade Tiramisu all around the table, and then paused behind Doc with her hands on his shoulders.

"Now that Doc and I have you all here and we're finally all enjoying this wonderful evening together, we have a surprise for you," Connie proclaimed.

"Oh bless the Lord, you're pregnant!" Marsha shouted and clapped her hands.

"Oh no, it's not that wonderful of a surprise," Connie laughed. "But we're working on it."

With that, Connie stepped to the buffet and took two envelopes from the top drawer. Then she sat beside Doc and handed the envelopes across the table to Madeleine and Marsha.

"Doc and I have been blessed mightily," she reiterated. "We have a beautiful home and a bright future. And the biggest reason for that has little to do with money...and everything to do with the wonderful friends you have become. Knowing that in our hearts and being prompted by God to share our blessings with those he has used to bless us, Doc and I want you to have and enjoy this gift from us…and from God."

Marsha opened her envelope first, gasped, showed Q the check inside, and burst into tears. Puzzled and excited, Madeleine slowly opened her envelope and peered inside. When she saw the amount on the check it contained, she was speechless. So she silently handed Noah the envelope. He opened it just wide enough to see the check, then silently sat back in his chair and stared at Doc.

"We can't…" Marsha started to say, before Connie interrupted her.

"Doc and I have had days of practice shooting down any objection you might be able to give us here at this table tonight," she said. "Nothing you could possibly say will change anything. So you're hereby officially stuck with just having been abundantly blessed by God through us, just as he has blessed us—and continues to bless us—through all of you. That's all there is to say. End of story. Period."

"Yeah…what she said…period!" Doc added to lighten the moment and to hear his dear friends' laughter.

"Dig in," Connie urged, "and let me know what you think of the dessert. It's a recipe I just got from a new friend of mine in town and I need to know if it's worth keeping."

When they'd finished dessert, the women drifted out to the patio to talk a bit about when they'd likely all have a chance to gather over the months ahead…now that they all could afford it. The men, meanwhile, headed to the study for Doc's promised time online. While Q settled in front of the keyboard and logged into his go-to federal data base, Doc gave Noah the rundown on the stranger Q had questioned suspiciously.

They sat far enough away to let Q enter any passwords and other identifying data, and watched him scroll through several different websites and hundreds of photos.

"This is often quite a cumbersome process," Q confirmed over his shoulder as he continued scrolling through photos. "Time can complicate it more than just about any other factor because Mother Nature—and the suspect's efforts to 'blend in'—can leave you looking for someone whose photo you have is now years older and may barely resemble their old self." Q saved the FBI's "Most Wanted Terrorist" website for last.

"Bingo!" Q yelled and raised his hands in the air. "Hello, Abdul Rahman Yasin! I found you, you slippery little son of a you-know-what! Your cousin, Khalid, refused to tell us where to find you. But like the stupid terrorist you are, you've stumbled right into our hands after all."

Yasin was wanted for his alleged role in the 1993 bombing of the World Trade Center, and he had a predictably long rap sheet:

- Damage by Means of Fire or an Explosive
- Damage by Means of Fire or an Explosive to United States Property
- Transport in Interstate Commerce an Explosive
- Destruction of Motor Vehicles or Motor Vehicle Facilities
- Conspiracy to Commit Offense or Defraud the United States

- Aiding and Abetting; Assault of a Federal Officer in the Line of Duty
- Commission of a Crime of Violence Through the Use of a Deadly Weapon or Device

"Are you sure that's the guy you saw in the gas station yesterday?" Doc asked.

"Absolutely!" Q declared. "There's no doubt in my mind. But what the heck is he doing cruising around the 'Middle-of-Nowhere' Montana?" Q questioned. "No offense to you, of course, Doc. In fact, you may be the reason he's here."

"Did you notice what type of vehicle he was driving, Q?" Doc asked.

"Of course," Q replied. "He rented a White Mustang GT Premium Fastback—Oxford. I've got the plate number and rental company in my head too."

"Showoff!" Doc chided him.

"Not bad for an old hunting dog, eh partner?" Q gloated.

"Not bad at all!" Noah said.

"But I don't know about this, Q," Doc hedged. "Are you positive it's Yasin? Why would he walk around town without a disguise?"

"Who knows why?" Q answered with a shrug. "Maybe he's just stupid, which would explain why he's being so careless in town? The only halfway logical explanation is that he knows you led the raid that captured his cousin and he's here for revenge."

"If that's true," Doc wondered out loud, "Homeland Security's got some serious leak problems."

"Ya think!" Doc vented.

"You have a point," Q agreed. "I'd better call the President directly."

Q got through to the President far faster than he would've guessed, especially at such a late hour. He kept the call short, related all the information he felt sure of, and told the President goodnight.

"Did you wake him?" Doc asked.

"Are you kidding?" Q laughed. "He's up with a few Secret Service gathered around, watching *Hellcats of the Navy*, starring none other than Ronald Reagan."

"President Reagan was in a movie?!" Noah asked, a little amazed and very confused.

"We'll explain in a bit," Q told him.

"I just knew the President was a fan of the Navy," Doc joked. "So what did he say about our visitor, Yasin?"

"He wanted to send security for us here, tonight," Q explained, "but I told him we didn't think that was necessary. He couldn't find you in broad daylight yesterday. I don't think he'll manage at this time of night. So the President is calling Border Security now to have them send a couple officers to watch the house as soon as they can get here."

"They'll be here by early morning from the Canadian border," Doc stated.

"You guys both told me it was calm and peaceful here," Noah reminded them with a chuckle.

"Things happen," Q sad with a shrug. "And remember, they always happen for a reason."

"And this could just be a false alarm," Doc added. "After all, the info is all coming from an old hunting dog."

"I don't understand," Noah questioned with a wrinkled brow.

"You will when you're older, son," Doc assured him.

"Now you sound just like my mother," Noah laughed.

"I tell him that all the time, and he really does," Q said and they all giggled.

22

PENULTIMATE

"Hey, do you want to see the neat gift Q gave me?" Doc asked Noah.

"Sure!" Noah said.

Doc led the men into the living room, took his new sword cane from its ornate box, and handed it to Noah.

"I remember this," Noah confirmed.

"He left the one you remember in Israel, Noah," Q explained. "The one you're holding is a replacement... only better. Press on the bottom of the anchor in the handle."

"Nice!" Noah confirmed quietly as he slid the etched, razor-sharp blade free from the barrel of the cane. "Very nice! And judging by what little I saw of your skills in my gym in Rome, I'd say you know how to handle this piece pretty well."

Noah slid the blade back inside the cane and handed it to Doc. Rather than placing the cane into the decorative box it came with, he carefully placed it across the arms of a padded chair for the night. Then he told his friends good-night and they all headed to bed.

Knowing Yasin was in the area wasn't enough to keep either Doc or Q awake that night, so they both were as rested and awake as Noah when they converged on the breakfast table. They'd enjoyed the smells of coffee and blueberry pancakes in the air since awaking. So they needed no prompting to move to the dining room that morning. The wives were a little suspicious when their men finished breakfast so fast and took their second cups of coffee out to the patio, so they could "talk."

"I wonder what that's all about?" Connie said softly.

"I hope it's not another mission," Marsha answered. "I told him last night before we went to sleep that I'd like him to retire."

"Well, for purely selfish reasons, I pray that he does, Marsha," Connie maintained. "Because I believe that would convince Doc to give it up, too."

"Then I pray along with both of you," Madeleine added, "because I'm positive Noah would rather hang out with your husbands than with anyone else...except for me, of course. So whatever they do, you can bet he'll be around them."

The men sat side by side on the patio with their bare feet up on the railing, enjoying the warm morning sun and the view of the lake stretching out for miles down below. It was almost 8 o'clock so Doc expected the two Border Patrol officers, promised by the President, would arrive soon.

"Marsha's right, Q, you do have big feet," Doc teased with a hearty laugh.

"Shut up, Doc," Q sighed.

"What are you guys talking about?" Noah was confused.

"Nothing," Doc said. "Nothing at all, Noah."

"Hey, Doc," Noah asked. "Do you mind if I bring that cane out here to take a good look at it in the sunlight?"

"Not at all, Noah," Doc answered. "Knock yourself out."

"Why would I do that?" Noah inquired.

"It's just an American expression, Noah. No need to panic," Q said with a hearty laugh.

Relieved, Noah brought the cane out and marveled at the workmanship.

"This is quite an impressive gift, Doc," Noah praised. "He must think the world of you."

"Oh, don't tell him that," Q said hurriedly. "You'll give him false hopes for Christmas."

A few minutes later, Noah set the cane on an unoccupied patio chair and resumed his position alongside his best friends, coffee cup in hand, feet on the railing. The conversation quickly turned to fishing and the trio let their guard down.

"Good morning, my fellow Americans," a voice with a thick Middle Eastern accent rang out close behind them.

All three men twisted in their chairs and caught sight of none other than Abdul Rahman Yasin standing in the center of the patio holding an AK-47.

"I knew I shoulda got a watchdog," Doc said, only half kidding.

"Which one of you is Captain John Holiday?" Yasin asked.

The trio looked at one another and feigned confusion.

"Uh, who?" Q inquired. "There's no one here by that name. Maybe you must have gotten the address wrong? It's very possible, you know. Remember how you lost once already?"

Yasin was growing impatient and angrier.

"I'm not stupid!" Yasin shouted at them. "Don't you be stupid either! Which of you is John Holiday?"

"Look at it this way." Doc took a turn at toying with the terrorist. "What difference does it really make? I mean, you're going to have to murder everybody here before you leave no matter what. So if Holiday is here, you're going to get him."

"I said shut up!" Yasin shouted. "I'm here to avenge my cousin, Khalid Mohammed Yasin, who your country is treating like a rabid animal. I want to look John Holiday in the eye when I kill him. I want him to know why I'm murdering him!"

"I'm sorry your cousin is being treated like a rabid animal, Yasin, old buddy," Q remarked. "But you see, that's how we treat rabid animals in America. And on that note, drop the hokey Middle Eastern accent. You were born in Bloomington, Indiana, for God's sake, which makes you every bit as much of an American as I am."

"By the way, Yasin," Doc chimed in again, "how are you feeling lately? Had any seizures lately? You know if your father would've kept the family in Indiana, instead of drag-ging butt to Iraq, you would've gotten good old American health care and better treatment for your epilepsy."

"That's enough, I said!" Yasin yelled even louder. "I'll kill you all!"

"What on earth's going on out here?" Marsha called out as she walked toward the trio with Madeleine and Connie following close behind.

"I'm John Holiday!" Doc shouted, knowing the danger had just increased exponentially.

What in the hell is taking Border Security so long to get here? Doc and Q were both thinking…and hoping they'd arrive in seconds.

"Get on your feet, John Holiday," Yasin shouted. "And die like a man!"

Doc did not move.

"I said stand up, you filthy dog!" Yasin bellowed even louder.

"Leave my husband alone!" Connie yelled. "Leave all of us alone! We've done nothing wrong, do you hear me?!"

"Perhaps if you won't stand up for yourself," Yasin taunted as he pointed the AK-47 at Connie, "you'll stand up for your beautiful wife."

"I'll stand," Doc agreed, sounding old and feeble. "But I need my cane to do it."

Yasin looked at the cane resting across the arms of a patio chair.

"Hand the dog his cane!" he screamed at Noah.

Noah leaned and stretched to grab the cane off the nearby chair and handed it to Doc.

"Thanks," Doc said quietly and gave Noah a wink.

Doc very convincingly struggled to get on his feet, and then leaned on the cane with both hands, seeming to put his full weight on it.

"Walk over here!" Yasin directed and waved the AK-47 in the direction of the patio steps leading to the beach.

Doc took slow, tentative steps, dragged his right foot, and slowly moved in the direction of the steps. When he got near Yasin, Doc pretended to lose his balance and stumble toward him. Then he grasped the ends of the cane with both hands and brought it up sharply under the barrel of Yasin's AK-47. The move caught the terrorist completely off guard, and he lost his balance and his grip on the weapon, which fell to the patio. Yasin then pulled a dagger and lunged at Doc using wild, rapid slashing and stabbing motions. Doc warded off every move with reflexes sharpened by the exercises and drills Noah had taught him at the HEMA training center in Rome.

Angered to have been caught so off guard, Yasin slashed and jabbed all the more wildly.

Doc felt himself tiring. He knew he must abandon his defensive strategy and bring the struggle to an end. With a single lightening-like motion Noah taught him, Doc jammed the cane into Yasin's ribs, pulled the sword from the cane's barrel, and pressed the tip tight against the underside of Yasin's chin.

"Please don't move a muscle," he whispered to Yasin while looking straight into his eyes, "or I'll have to run this blade right through your brain." Doc felt Yasin suddenly go limp. Then Doc saw the terrorist's eyes roll back in his head and foam began to ooze from the corners of his mouth. Next, his body began to shake and convulse and Doc could no longer hold him up.

"He's having a seizure!" Connie yelled and ran to the terrorist to help Doc hold his body securely in order to prevent him from injuring himself.

Noah saw the Border Security van barrel up the road to the house.

"Here they come!" he yelled excitedly and waved to them as a signal to hurry. Q quickly dialed 911 to summon an ambulance for Yasin.

The two officers quickly strapped Yasin to a stretcher and raced him to the hospital 20 minutes away.

"I'm ashamed to say part of me hopes they don't get to the hospital in time," Doc admitted.

"Don't be too hard on yourself, Doc," Q encouraged. "He's had seizures since childhood. So they must not be too serious."

"Actually, the one he just had might have saved his life," Doc exclaimed with a shudder. "I feared I was going to have to kill him."

"Why did he want to kill you, Doc?" Connie asked, fighting back tears. "Where did he come from? He's not from around here."

"Believe it or not, that was Abdul Rahmn Yasin," Doc revealed. "He's wanted by the FBI for the 1993 truck bombing of the World Trade Center."

"What a terrible human being," Connie uttered softly and wrapped herself in Doc's arms. "Are you sure you're alright, hon?"

"I am now," Doc said as he held her tight.

"How on earth did he ever show up here after being on the run all these years?" Marsha wondered out loud.

"He was upset about my role in the capture of one of his cousins who helped him make the Trade Center bombs," Doc explained. "The cousin was just sentenced for his part in the bombing, so I guess Abdul took it personally. The two major questions that need answers are: How did he connect me to his cousin's capture, and how did he find me? We'll never know."

"This is what I was talking about, Q, when I said Washington D.C. is a swamp," Doc explained. "I know our brand of service to the nation can be dangerous. I also realize the need for what we do is great and urgent. And I go to bed each night certain that I, and those around me, serve the best interests of our nation and its citizens. Too many people serving in D.C. can't say that...and I refuse to be one of them."

Doc's cell phone began ringing with a call from the White House.

Doc gave everyone a sly grin and said, "He must be listening."

"Good evening. Is this Captain John H. Holiday?" a friendly woman's voice asked.

"Yes it is," Doc replied.

"Please stand by for the President," she advised and placed him on hold.

"Hello, Doc!" the President's voice boomed at Doc's end.

"Hello Mr. President," Doc replied. "How are you this evening?"

"Wonderful, just wonderful, Doc," the President revealed enthusiastically. "I just had to call and thank you. I've received word that we have Abdul Rahmn Yasin in custody, thanks to you and your team there in Washington."

"Yes, sir, we were just debriefing here at my home, Mr. President," Doc said and smiled at everyone on the patio. "It's good to know you're being kept informed so well and so fast."

"I'm guessing you know there is a $5 million reward for information leading to the arrest of that sack of sand, and I was hoping you'd be able and willing to pick up the check personally here at the White House in the next day or two. I'd love to see you and Connie again."

"I'm confident we can make that happen, Mr. President," Doc replied.

"Great! So I'll look forward to seeing the two of you," the President proclaimed. "I'll have my staff fax you a menu, so you can let them know when to expect you and what the two of you would like for lunch."

"I'm sure Connie will be thrilled with the choices, Mr. President."

"Good! Good! It was wonderful to hear your voice again, Doc."

"Likewise, Mr. President," Doc replied.

"Oh, Doc!" The president suggested, "While you're here, I also have a small matter I'd like to discuss with you. So plan to be here just a little longer than luncheon meetings normally take."

"I'll let Connie know as well, Mr. President," Doc agreed. "Thanks again for calling."

"Goodbye and God bless, Doc," the President said and ended the call.

"A personal 'thank you' is always nice," Connie said and flashed Doc a proud smile.

"Sure is!" Doc agreed. "And a $5 million reward is even nicer!"

"What?!" Connie gasped. "Oh, thank you, Lord in heaven!"

Doc joined Connie, Q, Marsha, Noah, and Madeleine in jumping and cheering.

"Looks like we have to write you folks another check," John laughed as he spread his arms as wide as he could and shouted, "Group hug!"

EPILOGUE

The warm comfort that filled Doc's heart as the Escalade pulled up to the North Entrance of the White House made him smile. As the Secret Service agent hopped out to open the rear door, Doc squeezed Connie's hand in his special way that signaled his gratitude for having her in his life.

The President and Melanie were laughing as they appeared in the dining room. They were grateful to finally share a meal with guests brave enough to write "grilled cheese and tomato soup" on the White House menu.

"Connie, I knew you were courageous when you accepted Doc's proposal of marriage," the President chuckled. "But your note on the menu clinched it for me. You two are truly an awesome couple and Melanie and I count it a privilege to have you as friends."

"The feeling is mutual for Connie and me, Mr. President," Doc replied. "Feeling as we do that public service is a privilege, it's overwhelming to be recognized for our service in such heartfelt ways. Our friendship with you and the first lady is among our greatest blessings."

"With all that said and out of the way," the President continued, "here's the check I mentioned during my call to thank you for your role in ending Mr. Yasin's threat to our nation."

"Well, we're happy to inform you that after discussing the matter with those who played key roles in Yasin's arrest, we've decided to donate the reward to the Disabled American Veterans. I'm sure you can make that happen in the most effective way, Mr. President."

"And you can bet I will," the President concurred as he slipped the check into his breast pocket. "You folks are the greatest. That's why I take such comfort in making my next request. We seized a number of documents from Mr. Yasin's rental car. Of particular interest is one that refers to something called the Guardians of the Forbidden Library. To be completely honest with you, what little we've been able to uncover has us greatly worried for two major reasons: The first one is that the story is so incredible it could be highly embarrassing for our intelligence community to expend money and resources, only to find out that it's pure fantasy. The second reason is that if the story is true, the entire world may well hang in the balance."

"I guess this is where I quietly say, tell me more," Doc expressed.

"I would if I could, Doc," the President replied. "But I really can't divulge any more without your explicit agreement to accept the mission."

"Then this is where I say I'll make some phone calls and get back to you as soon as possible," Doc promised.

"I'm really sorry to offer this during what I'd hoped would be a laid back time to enjoy each other's company," the President said apologetically. "But I got the call about this just before Melanie came and got me for lunch."

"It's completely alright, Mr. President," Doc confirmed as he glanced at Connie and squeezed her hand in his special way, then turned back to the President and said just what Connie expected. "Everything happens for a reason."

THE END

Printed in the USA
CPSIA information can be obtained
at www.ICGtesting.com
LVHW022133221023
761835LV00026B/533

9 798605 791751